BOX SET NOVELLAS 1-3

LARSON SISTERS
SERIES

Karen Baney

desert life
media

Larson Sisters Series: Box Set Novellas 1-3
By Karen Baney

Publisher:
Desert Life Media, LLC
Gilbert, AZ 85295

www.karenbaney.com

Printed in the United States of America

ISBN-978-1-960217-65-3

IN LOVE
AT
CHRISTMAS

I lift up my eyes to the hills,
From where does my help come?
My help comes from the Lord,
Who made heaven and earth.

—*Psalm 121:1-2*

CHAPTER I

Larson Stables
Near Prescott, Arizona Territory
September 21, 1886

CATY

"CATY, WAKE UP."

I groaned and rolled over.

"Come on."

Two pairs of hands shook me.

"Let's go," Penny said as she tugged me until I sat up.

"Come. On." Dory whined.

"Fine. I'm up."

"Here." Penny thrust my coat toward me. "Put this on."

After I wiped the sleepy sand from my eyes, I donned my coat and boots as my sisters dragged me out of the house toward the lake. It had been years since the three of us went to the dock to gaze at the stars. My twentieth birthday was a good time to resurrect the stargazing tradition.

"Watch your step," Dory warned as she held up the lantern.

I carefully stepped onto the dock and walked to the other end before I sat down. Penny sat next to me, and Dory sat on her other side. Then the three of us laid on our backs and snuggled close to keep warm while we looked up at the stars. Slowly, I let out a long breath as I drank in the beauty of a million stars twinkling overhead. So peaceful.

"Turn down the lantern," Penny said.

Dory giggled as she extinguished it. "It's been too long."

"I know," Penny said. "I miss this. One day, we won't be able to do this anymore."

A twinge of sadness washed over me. At seventeen, Penny had already turned the heads of several boys at church. Her light blue eyes and wild brown curly hair enhanced her natural beauty. She might marry before me, if it wasn't for her singular focus on one particular boy.

"Caty, what is your dream? Has it changed?" Dory asked. At fourteen, marriage still seemed like a distant dream for my youngest sister. Though her figure started filling out her dresses. In another year or two, she'd be considered a fine catch.

With the dawn of my twentieth birthday, I doubted God would grant me the desires of my heart. I had only one.

"To marry a craftsman," I whispered the words. I knew it was an odd request, but it was my heart's truest desire.

"Still?" Penny asked.

"What do you mean by craftsman?" Dory asked.

"A man with some talent. Woodworking or something like that. He makes beautiful things out of ordinary things."

"Kinda like Papa does when he whittles figurines?" Dory asked.

"Only on a larger scale."

Soon enough, I'd have to abandon my dream if it didn't come true. Perhaps my dream was unattainable. Or perhaps I wasn't pretty enough to gain any man's attention. Twenty inched closer to spinsterhood. Some might already consider me that.

"What about you, Penny?" I asked.

She laughed. "To marry Nathan Cahill, silly. It's my one and only goal in life."

As I figured, her answer remained unchanged. For years, she said the same thing. Always our cousin Nathan. Not that he was related by blood. His mother's first husband had been Mama's oldest brother. After he passed, she married another man, Nathan's father. So even though we grew up calling him cousin, only his older brother and sister actually were.

"Has he noticed you yet?" Dory asked.

Penny let out a long breath. "We're best friends. But no. He has not noticed me romantically. We still have time."

A smile stretched across my lips. So true.

"And you, Dory?" Penny asked.

"I think I want to marry a man just like Papa. Handsome. Gifted with horses."

Her dream made the most sense. Our papa, Adam Larson, earned the respect of every man he met. His reputation for breeding and training horses stretched far across the territory. He loved our mama deeply, even after more than twenty years of marriage. That was the kind of love I longed for. Deep. Abiding.

"You couldn't pick a better kind of man to dream about," I said.

"I want a godly man," she added.

"Don't we all?" Penny asked.

"I certainly do," I replied.

Our words faded as we each gazed at the stars overhead. I prayed, thanking God for His masterpiece of the beautiful night sky. *Please, Lord, let me fall in love soon. If the man you have for me isn't a craftsman, I'll let that dream go. I yearn for a godly man who will love me.*

Penny's breathing slowed, and a snore escaped her lips. I

nudged her, annoyed she fell asleep before we brought our outing to a close.

"Dory, will you pray?" I asked.

"Lord, we ask, if it is Your Will, bring a craftsman for Caty. Let Nathan Cahill fall madly in love with Penny. When I am older, bring a man like Papa for me."

"Amen," Penny and I whispered.

We sat up before we hurried back to our warm beds.

This year. Maybe it would be my year.

CHAPTER 2

Prescott, Arizona Territory
December 22, 1886

JOSIAH

AFTER ANOTHER LATE night, I rolled off the cot in my workshop. It was the first December I owned a store, and I underestimated the amount of last-minute business that came in before the holiday.

The stove barely emitted any heat. I tossed more wood in its belly. Then I prepared the coffeepot. Mama would be upset I'd not come home again. She'd be by soon to check on me and bring breakfast. I hoped.

I ran a hand through my hair. Since I had no mirror, I did not know how scruffy I looked. My itchy beard irritated me, but I left my shaving kit at home. I washed up and donned a fresh change of clothes. Knowing Mama, she'd bring me something clean again today. She was so good to me.

After I tied my laces, I poured a cup of coffee. Then I entered the main part of the store. The clock read five after nine. Good. I wasn't too late. I turned the sign to "open." Then I chugged my coffee and returned to my workshop.

The large cedar-lined wardrobe Mr. Murphy ordered stood near the doorway. I assembled it last night, but still needed to sand it, add some carved decorative touches, stain it, and lacquer it. Unfortunately, it would be late in the day before I could get to it. There were so many other orders waiting to be filled.

I smiled as I pictured a few of Santa's elves coming to help me. I sure could use some help. Probably should ask my stepfather. He would if I asked. Yet something held me back. I wanted to prove I could manage my shop without my parents.

As I contemplated carving decorative touches on another customer's jewelry box, I thought about my morning prayers. I longed for a woman who would appreciate my work. I hoped she would admire it. Woodworking combined both skill and art, at least it did for me. Any woman interested in me would have to understand that. Especially during lean times.

Some men wanted a wife to cook and clean. I wanted a kindhearted, godly woman who would see the beauty in the things I created. A woman to come alongside me. I had no clearer picture of what that truly meant or how God might choose to bring her into my life.

As I sat on the bench, I picked up the pieces of the rocking horse I cut last night. They needed sanded. When the bell over the door rang, I set the pieces aside and entered the main room.

"Mama." I greeted her with a kiss on the cheek.

"Josiah, I declare you look exhausted." Worry clouded her dark brown eyes as her lower lip protruded in a pout.

Even after living in Prescott for more than a decade, Mama's southern accent remained fully intact. Mine faded to a bit of a drawl in some words, much to her disappointment.

"I brought you some sweet tea. Here's a plate of breakfast. I've wrapped up a few sandwiches for later," she said as she bustled to my workshop in the back. She set the sandwiches and tea on a counter.

"Thank you."

When she turned toward me, she placed a hand on my face. Heat warmed my cheeks. I was a twenty-four-year-old man. Thankfully, no one walked in front of the shop to see the motherly gesture. Her hand returned to her side.

"Please try to come home for supper."

"I don't know."

"Josiah."

Her tone held a warning, one I'd ignore in favor of completing the orders due tomorrow and the next day. She handed me the plate full of eggs, bacon, sausage, and grits. Then she walked past me and studied the wardrobe for Mrs. Murphy.

"This looks lovely," she said. "Will you carve some roses for the cornice?"

"Yes, with some vining stems and leaves."

"Mrs. Murphy will love it, I am sure. I hope Mr. Murphy is paying you well."

I gave her a half smile. "More than well. He doubled my fee for expediting it."

"I am proud of you, son."

I kissed her cheek before I escorted her to the door. Then I scarfed down breakfast. After setting the plate aside, I went back to work.

Some time later, the bell rang again. I greeted a customer and showed him the jewelry box he had commissioned. After a few minutes of praise, he finally left. I appreciated his sentiments, but the amount of work left undone overwhelmed me.

When I returned to the workshop, the bell rang again before I sat down. I let out a loud sigh. Maybe I ought to close the store so I could finish the orders I'd already accepted.

I stepped into the shop. A woman faced the coat rack. She shimmied her arms and her coat slid down to her waiting hands, revealing her slender figure. My throat went dry. I thought it might be Caty Larson. She occupied my thoughts more often lately, though I had yet to summon the courage to even speak to her at church.

As she turned around, my breath caught. It was indeed Caty. She wore a lovely purple silk dress which highlighted every bit of her femininity. Her golden locks rested in a coil at the base of her soft neck. The lace edging the collar drew my eyes up to the lace on the matching hat. Her green eyes lit when she saw me. She looked even more beautiful than I remembered. It was the closest I'd ever stood to her. Then she smiled at me, and my heart pommeled my chest. I cleared my throat as she approached me.

"Mr. Elliot." She said my name as if it were a gift. "I need your help."

My stomach tightened. I didn't have time to accept any more orders for Christmas. Yet, I could not bear to disappoint her or cause her sweet smile to disappear.

"Miss Larson," I greeted her.

"Please, call me Catherine. Or better yet, Caty. All my friends do."

"Caty, I'm sorry—"

"There is plenty of time to finish the piece I want you to make. It's for my mother's birthday the third week of January."

I straightened as the weight lightened from my shoulders. "How can I help?"

"May I call you Josiah?"

I beamed. "I'd like that."

She stepped closer and unfolded a piece of paper. "Josiah, this is a special birthday for Mama. I thought," she said as she smoothed the paper flat, "that she would like a special box for some keepsakes from her mother and treasures from myself and my sisters over the years."

Though it was difficult, I tore my eyes away from her lovely green ones to study the paper.

"How large were you thinking?" I asked.

"Larger than a jewelry box, but smaller than a chest. Have you anything like it?"

I led her over to a display case with many sizes of jewelry boxes. "Do any of these look like the size you wanted?"

She perused the boxes. As she reached for one, she quickly drew back her hand as if she should not touch it. I picked it up and handed it to her.

"You may look at them closer."

Pink tinged her cheeks when she took the box from me. I caught a whiff of her fragrance, which smelled like spring flowers. Then I thought if I could smell her, she might smell me, which might not be so pleasant. So I took a step back.

Caty ran her slender fingers over the carvings on the top of the box. "This is beautiful." Her index finger traced the scrolled pattern I had carved. "How long does something like this take?"

My heart warmed at the admiration in her tone. "A few hours to carve it. Then I sand it smooth. Stain it."

When she glanced up, her eyes connected with mine. My pulse quickened as she handed the box back to me. Her fingers brushed against mine, accidentally, I thought. Trails of warmth spread from her touch. I must find the courage to ask her to have a meal with me. Or something. Anything to get to know her better.

CHAPTER 3

CATY

When Josiah's hand touched mine, tingles traveled up my arm. With a day's growth of beard on his chin and his mussed hair, he looked roguishly handsome. His deep blue eyes shimmered with interest. My breath caught, and I quickly released the jewelry box from my hand.

As my pulse raced, I said, "That one is smaller than I had in mind." Then I described the keepsakes Mama had. A broach from her mother. Some drawings from Penny. Handcrafted holiday ornaments from Dory. Papa's love notes.

"I see. I think…" He held up one finger before he hurried to the back room. Then he returned with some wood scraps of different sizes. He held two of them together. "Something about this size?"

Excitement washed over me. "Yes, that's perfect."

His warm and inviting smile made my heart flutter.

"May I keep your drawing?"

"Of course."

He set the scrap wood aside. After he pulled a pencil from his pocket, he jotted some notes on the paper.

"Would you like a design on the box?"

"Mama loves horses. Larson Stables, you know."

He laughed. "I should hope so. I can carve a galloping horse on the top. Or scrollwork, vines, flowers, pretty much anything."

I placed a hand at my throat. "You can carve a galloping horse?"

Josiah nodded. "I have something similar over here."

He motioned me to follow him to another section of the store. My breath shallowed when I saw the intricate work. My fingers glided over the smooth surface.

"Does this cost more?"

"What's your budget?"

I told him. Then he smiled, and warmth settled in my belly.

"For that price, I could do something similar."

Once we completed the arrangements, I found myself reluctant to leave his store, as I so enjoyed seeing his creations. The clock on his wall chimed one o'clock, drawing his attention away.

"I…" He glanced at the workshop, then at me. His lips parted several times. At length, he finally asked, "Have you eaten? My mother brought several sandwiches by and I would be happy to share one with you."

Heat warmed my cheeks. "I would like that."

"Just let me dust off a chair. I wouldn't want to ruin your stunning dress."

How incredibly sweet. A few minutes later, he escorted me to the back room. Two plates sat at the end of his workshop table. A blanket draped over one chair, which he held out for me. Then he sat in the chair across from me.

I smiled as he poured some tea.

"It's sweet tea," he said as he set it in front of me.

I took a sip and smiled. "It's good."

When he held out his palm toward me, I slipped my dainty

hand into his. His callused fingers curled around mine. Then he bowed his head. I did the same as he prayed for the simple meal. Once the prayer ended, he released my hand.

We talked as we ate the simple meal together. His smile lit his eyes and warmed my soul. I wondered why the two of us had not spoken before. We never ran out of things to talk about.

Then the clock struck half-past two. His smile faded as he stood.

"I hate to—"

"I ought to head back home now," I said. "I'm so sorry to have kept you from your work."

He led me to the front room. He took my hand in his as he gazed into my eyes. "I'm not sorry. I really enjoyed the time with you, Caty."

The way he said my name felt like the first warm breeze on a spring day. I truly did not want to leave. But I knew I kept him from a mountain of work. Then an idea formed.

"What can I do to help?" I asked.

Josiah's eyes traveled from my head to my feet. "I would not want you to ruin your dress."

"Do you have an apron?"

He looked up at the corner of the room. Then his face lit up. "I do."

When he returned from the workshop, he held out a manly canvas apron. I giggled. "That will work. Show me what to do."

Then he showed me how to sand. He retrieved the parts of a rocking horse before he placed a sandpaper block on the flat surface. Once I grasped it, Josiah stood next to me and covered my hand with his. I liked the feel of it and the tingles that ran up my arm. He led me in the motion of sanding the wood while his other hand rested lightly on my waist. His nearness thrilled me. For several seconds, his hand remained over mine.

When the motion stopped, I noticed everything about him. The strength of his hands. The warmth of him standing so close. I glanced up at him and smiled. His face was only inches from mine.

He cleared his throat and released his hold as he stepped back. He hurried to the other side of the table.

"You're a natural," he said. "When the wood feels soft to the touch, then it's ready."

I nodded and watched as he turned his attention to a large plank of wood. He measured and marked off lengths of it. Then he cut it. I could watch him all day.

Shaking my head, I focused on sanding the rocking horse pieces. I moved on to the next one after the first felt smooth. We worked in companionable silence for hours.

Before I realized it, the sun lowered in the sky. I was in danger of not making it back home for supper if I didn't leave immediately.

"Thank you for your help," Josiah said, as he held my coat for me. "Are you sure you don't want me to accompany you home?"

"No, I've already taken up far too much of your time to-day. I'll be fine."

"I really enjoyed spending time with you, Caty."

I squeezed his hand before I darted out of the shop. Then I climbed on my horse and headed home with a heart full of joy.

The next morning, I baked a batch of gingersnap cookies. The moment they cooled, I placed them in a tin. Then I packed two dresses in a valise. I took the valise and cookies with me to the barn.

Papa asked where I was going as I put my things on my horse. I realized I should have probably asked permission since I still lived in his home. Though he gave me plenty of freedom.

"I'm going to stay with Aunt Caroline and come back on Christmas morning with her family."

Papa raised an eyebrow.

"Will that be alright? We have the caroling tomorrow after Christmas Eve service. And I promised to help her bake today."

He leaned forward and placed a kiss on my cheek. Then he winked at me. "I suppose you've left me to tell your mother?"

I grinned before I mounted my horse. "Love you, Papa!" Then I kicked my horse toward town as his chuckling faded behind me.

When I arrived in town, I noticed that Josiah's shop was open, so I pulled up in front of it before I dismounted and tied my horse outside. I entered the room as the bell clinked overhead.

"Just a minute!" Josiah called from his workshop.

While I waited, I smiled and recalled the feel of his hand on mine as he showed me how to sand the rocking horse yesterday evening. I perused the many beautiful creations lining the shelves of his shop. The detail of the carvings amazed me. He was incredibly gifted.

"Caty?" The astonishment in his voice warmed my heart as I turned to face him.

A light laugh escaped my lips at the sight of his disheveled hair and stormy eyes. "I promise I won't monopolize your day. I apologize for taking so much of your time yesterday, so I brought you these."

A smile slowly stretched across his lips as he moved closer. He accepted the tin of cookies before he clasped my hand for a few seconds as he spoke.

"There's nothing to apologize for. The time I spent with you was delightful."

Tingles wiggled their way into my heart as he let go of my hand. His eyes revealed the sincerity of his words. At that moment, I was twice as glad I baked the cookies for him.

"Would it be rude for me to open this now?" he asked sheepishly.

"Please do."

When he opened the tin, he breathed deeply. "Gingersnap. My favorite."

"Are they? You're not just being kind?"

"They are." As he took one and chomped down on it, his eyes closed, savoring the cookie. "This is delicious. Dare I say, better than Mama's?"

"That is high praise indeed."

"Thank you, Caty."

Heat warmed my cheeks, so I turned my attention toward the many creations on the shelves. "Are these commissioned by customers?"

I heard the soft clank of the metal tin as he set it on a counter before he stood next to me.

"These two shelves are items customers should pick up today or tomorrow. The items in the case below are things I've made that I think customers might like. Perhaps I'll have a few last-minute shoppers stop by today."

"Do you need someone to manage the store? Don't you have a lot of orders left to complete?"

"Thank you for the kind offer. My sister Constance is going to help today and tomorrow."

"Constance Quinn is your sister?"

"Half-sister, yes."

"She's planning on caroling with us tomorrow night. She has quite a lovely voice."

"Mama would be proud to hear you say that."

"Well, I best be off. I promised my Aunt Caroline I'd help bake cookies for the carolers."

"If you make more gingersnap cookies, then the carolers are

in for a treat."

As I held the door open, he added, "Thanks again, Caty."

"You're welcome," I replied as I hurried from the store.

CHAPTER 4

JOSIAH

FOR THE BETTER part of two days, I daydreamed about Caty Larson as I worked hard to finish all the orders. Those ginger-snap cookies had been cooked to perfection. I rationed them and each time I ate one, I thought about her.

On Christmas Eve day, I woke before dawn and still had a long way to go before I would finish everything I'd promised. I glanced at the rocking horse Caty sanded for me and I wished I had her help. I smiled as I thought about the way she bit her lower lip when she concentrated on the work. She and I worked well together. Something I'd given up hope of finding.

Perhaps she was the woman I'd prayed for. She loved the Lord. She helped others, like baking cookies for me or for the Christmas carolers. I'd seen her every week at church, sitting with her family. She always had a smile at the ready.

After running a hand through my hair, I tried to push thoughts of her from my mind. Though the thoughts were pleasant and I longed to linger on them, they slowed me down. I had to stain Mr. Murphy's wardrobe in the next hour so it'd dry with enough time to lacquer it before I slept.

I grabbed a soft cloth and dipped it into the dark stain. Then

I rubbed it over the surface of the piece. As the stain soaked into the wood, the beauty of the grain multiplied. The stain also brought the decorative rose carvings to life. It was one of the finest pieces of furniture I'd made.

Thankfully, Constance agreed to help all day. I heard the bell ring often as the steady stream of customers came to pick up the gifts for their loved ones. More than once, I heard a customer express their joy over my craftsmanship. It affirmed that opening the shop had been an excellent decision. It humbled me to use my God-given talents to help others.

Right as I finished staining the Murphy's wardrobe, Mama stopped by with a late lunch.

"What's this?" she asked as she touched the cookie tin from Caty.

Heat warmed my neck and face as I washed my hands. "It's from Caty Larson."

"Oh? I did not know you were well acquainted with her."

"I'm not. Or wasn't." I sighed as I sat at the table, since Mama clearly intended to eat her lunch with me. "She stopped by to commission a keepsake box for January. When she saw how much work I had, she volunteered to help. So I showed her how to sand."

Mama's eyes rounded. "You put the young lady to work?"

"It's not like that. She asked if she could help. She seemed eager to."

Her arched eyebrows lowered as a smile slowly spread across her face. "I see."

I quickly prayed and stuffed a spoonful of stew in my mouth before Mama could draw more information from me. Or so I thought.

"And she brought you cookies today?"

I shook my head. I was not ready to say anything to Mama about Caty.

"She brought them yesterday," Constance said. I glared at my little sister. "He won't even let me try one."

"What kind are they?"

"Gingersnap," Constance said.

I really wished she'd spend more time eating than tattling.

"Well, Caty made more for after service tonight," Mama said as she patted my sister's hand, "so, you'll get to try one then."

"Do you think you'll make it home for supper tonight?" she asked me.

"I doubt it. I still have to lacquer Mr. Murphy's wardrobe so it will dry before tomorrow morning."

"Is he picking it up?"

"No. I need to deliver it by noon."

"I'll let your father know. Perhaps Caroline's boys can help."

"Thanks Mama, for everything. I need to return to work."

Graciously, she stayed until the dishes were clean. She set a fresh change of clothes for me on the cot. "I brought your shaving kit. We'll see you at service tonight?"

I nodded before she kissed my cheek and left.

The hours flew by and I worked as fast as I could without sacrificing the quality of my workmanship. At six o'clock, I stopped and cleaned up for service at half-past six. I rushed through shaving and nicked myself twice. But I arrived at church and slid into my family's pew as the opening refrains of the first hymn rang out.

Boughs of pine garland and red velvet ribbons lined the edge of each pew. Candelabras at the front cast a golden glow over the room. The smell of cinnamon and spice hung in the air. All of it felt like Christmas.

I glanced toward the Larson's pew. Caty looked divine in a rich burgundy gown. She peeked over her shoulder and smiled when she caught me staring. The dress brought out the green color of her eyes, stealing away my breath. In just a few short days, she wormed her way deep into my heart.

When the next song started, I forced my attention to the service and reverently celebrated Christ's birth and the salvation He offered. Pastor kept the service simple by reading the Christmas story from Luke before we sang *Silent Night* to close the service.

Once the service concluded, I regretted the need to return to work. I wished I could socialize with my peers. I would have loved to spend more time with Caty with nothing urgent pulling me away. Or to enjoy the cookies she baked. Or go caroling with her on my arm.

As I headed toward the door, she caught up to me.

"Josiah, wait." Her soft touch on my arm stopped me. I turned toward her and waited for her to speak.

"Do you still have more work?"

"Unfortunately, yes. It's likely to be a late night for me."

I saw her disappointment before she masked it. Then she smiled. "Merry Christmas."

"Merry Christmas," I said before I took her hand in mine. As I placed a light kiss on it, rosy circles graced her cheeks. Reluctantly, I released her hand. "I hope to see you soon."

"I'd like that."

Then I turned and left her sweet presence. I vowed I would take her on an outing soon. She was far too wonderful to let her get away.

As I walked back toward the shop, a light dusting of snow fell from the sky. The streetlights glowed yellow. They had decorated each with pine boughs and red ribbons. Everything about the walk reminded me of Christmas and just how much I'd missed this year.

CHAPTER 5

CATY

MY FACE STILL felt warm when I turned back to my sisters and friends. Josiah kissed my hand, and it was marvelous. The tingles that radiated from his touch made me feel special.

"Have you found your craftsman?" Dory whispered as she looped her hand around my arm.

Heat warmed my cheeks again. "Perhaps."

"Tell us about him," Penny said.

"There's not much to tell. I met him two days ago in his shop. Then he offered to share his lunch with me. He had so much work to do, that I stayed to help."

"Constance said you baked cookies for him," Dory said. "That sounds serious."

I glanced down before I looked back up, grinning. "Maybe."

Penny squealed.

"Shh!" I warned her.

After twenty minutes of sipping hot cocoa and snacking on baked goods, Aunt Caroline organized the carolers. When she discussed the route we would take through town, I interrupted her.

"I thought we could stop at Josiah, er, Mr. Elliot's shop first," I said. "He's been working very hard to complete a few projects before morning. He could use a little holiday cheer."

"What an excellent idea!" Aunt Caroline exclaimed. "That's near to the first house on our route."

"Is he your beau?" Penny nudged me.

"I hardly know him."

She snorted and looped her arm around mine as we left the church.

The light snowfall added a dreamy quality to the still town. Everything in the crisp air felt like Christmas.

"He's quite handsome," Dory said. "The two of you would make a lovely couple."

"I couldn't agree more," Aunt Caroline said. "If he's a smart man, he'll not waste this opportunity."

My heart warmed, and hope grew in my soul.

When we arrived at Josiah's shop, I noticed the back door propped open and pointed it out to Aunt Caroline. She asked us to line up just outside the door. Then she arranged us in three rows. The taller people in the back, like my cousin Deacon. Then the other adults in the middle. The shorter folks and teenagers were in the front, including Josiah's sister Constance.

"Let's start with O Little Town of Bethlehem, then Joy to The World."

"My brother likes We Three Kings," Constance said.

"Perfect. We'll end with that," Aunt Caroline said.

Then she raised her arms and counted time as we started singing.

Josiah pushed his door open and smiled when he saw me. I tried to smile back while I sang the songs. His eyes only briefly darted away from mine to take in the carolers before they returned to mine. His attention brought another blush to my cheeks. I enjoyed looking at him as much as he seemed to enjoy looking at me.

He had changed since he left the Christmas Eve service. His canvas apron covered tan trousers and a cream-colored shirt. Bits of sawdust rested in his dark locks. Those deep blue eyes shone with gratitude, making me very glad I suggested we stop by.

When we started singing *We Three Kings*, his smile grew wider and his foot tapped against the floor of his workshop. As the last strain came to a close, my feet rooted to the ground. I glanced at Penny, and she gave me a knowing smile.

"We'll see you tomorrow," Penny said. "Enjoy a few moments with your beau."

Josiah waved and thanked the carolers. "You best hurry or you'll miss out on the caroling."

"That's alright."

My pulse sped up as his eyes remained fixed on mine. I could fall into those eyes forever.

JOSIAH

WHEN I ENTERED the back of the workshop, I propped the door open despite the chilly air. The smell of the lacquer overpowered the small space, and I preferred allowing some fresh air in the room while I worked with it.

I changed back into my work clothes, donned my canvas apron, and set about brushing the smelly substance on the surface of the Murphy's wardrobe. As I worked, I admired the large piece of furniture. Mrs. Murphy loved roses, and I thought she'd appreciate the detail of the petals I carved into the wood.

Suddenly, the strains of *O Little Town of Bethlehem* sounded from behind me. I turned to peer out the door. There stood the carolers from the church. Caty smiled at me, as much as one could smile and still sing.

I returned her smile before I gave the singers my full attention, though my gaze remained fixed on Caty. The carolers sang two more songs, including my favorite, before they left.

Except Caty lingered. Her soft smile warmed my heart. The cold air caused cute pink splotches to rest on her cheeks. Her lips looked red and inviting, a thought which caused my breath to lodge in my throat.

"Have you eaten any supper?" she asked, bringing my thoughts back to reality.

I shook my head. "Too much to do."

"Let me fix something for you at my aunt's house. I'll be back soon."

Before I could respond, she darted away. *What a wonderful, thoughtful woman*, I thought before I went back to work.

CHAPTER 6

CATY

WHEN I ASKED Josiah if he had eaten, I figured he had not and was delighted that I already set aside a plate for him back at Aunt Caroline's. I rushed to her home, retrieved the plate and some pie for both of us. I hoped my sisters and friends would forgive me for abandoning them in the middle of caroling.

Once I arrived back at Josiah's shop, I rounded the building to the back door, still propped open. I knocked as I pushed it open.

"I'm back," I announced, startling him.

"Let me take that from you."

When his fingers lightly brushed my arm, those dreamy tingles shot to my heart. I wondered if it was appropriate to dine with the man alone at night. But he needed a meal and more help, judging by the state of his workshop.

He quickly brushed the sawdust from a chair and held it for me.

"You have been quite good to me this week," he said after he prayed for the meal.

My cheeks warmed as I studied his clean-shaven face. He looked even more handsome with the stubble removed. For the first time, I noticed the darling dimple in his chin.

"It's nothing."

"No, don't say that. I truly appreciate all you've done. And I suspect you haven't been helping all the shop owners on the street."

My face flamed as he winked at me. "No, just you," I whispered.

When he finished his meal, I pushed a slice of pie across the table to him. Then I took a bite of mine. The tartness of the apples made me smile.

"Did you bake this too?"

I nodded. "Apple is my favorite."

"Mine too."

Despite the cool breeze from the propped open door, I felt suddenly warm. Without knowing it, I brought him his favorite cookies and pie in a few short days. As I studied him, his eyes roamed over my face until they connected with mine again. It seemed like I'd known him for years. We grew very comfortable around each other in such a short timeframe. I wondered if he felt the same.

"How late will you need to work?" I asked.

He shrugged. "Until everything is done. No one wants a late Christmas gift."

"Do you need more help?" I asked before I thought twice or considered how inappropriate it might be.

"I… I could use help, but I ought to send you home. It's rather late and I don't want to ruin your lovely dress."

Then he grinned. "If you are going to keep helping a woodworker, you should not wear nice clothes."

I laughed. "I'll run back to Aunt Caroline's and change. She'll want to know where I am."

"Alright. I'll understand if you decide not to come back."

"I'm a woman of my word, Josiah."

My eyes locked with his for a few seconds before I gathered the plates I brought over, then I hurried back to Aunt Caroline's. My cousin Lily helped me out of the gorgeous Christmas dress. Then I donned the dress I wore for the baking yesterday. I brushed off the traces of flour before I put on my coat.

"Where are you going?" Uncle Thomas asked.

"I'm going to help Josiah finish up a few orders for his customers."

He narrowed his eyes, but Aunt Caroline laid a hand on his shoulder.

"It's Christmas Eve. Let her go."

Uncle Thomas glanced at the clock. "If you're not back by midnight, then I'm sending Drew after you."

"Thank you!" I beamed as I dashed out of their home. I heard my aunt's laughter behind me. Thank goodness she was such a romantic.

When I returned to Josiah's shop, he put me to work sanding a cedar trunk. We chatted while we worked.

"Will this need stained?" I thought he might not have time for things to dry.

"No. On a trunk like that, I finish it by oiling the wood, which dries quickly. That's why I saved several similar items for tonight."

"Smart."

He grinned. "Shall I show you how to oil it?"

I nodded.

Then he took a bottle of lemon oil and poured it onto a soft cloth. He stroked the top of the trunk in the same direction as the wood grain, which I learned was very important to every task in woodworking.

When he handed me the cloth and oil, I took it.

"Like this?" I asked as I dabbed more oil on the cloth.

"Perfect. We'll make you a craftsman yet."

His choice of word landed on my heart like the soft breeze on a summer's day. Craftsman. Could he be the man I'd prayed for?

I glanced down and rubbed the soft cloth against the trunk.

"Oh!" I exclaimed as the richness of the woodgrain emerged before my very eyes. "It's exquisite."

When I looked back up at him, he watched me. His eyes shone with something I could not place before he turned his attention back to the massive wardrobe. I bit my lower lip as I blotted more oil on the cloth and ran it along the grain. Within the hour, I finished the trunk and moved on to the next item.

At eleven o'clock, Josiah stretched as he backed away from the wardrobe.

"Is it done?" I asked as I stood beside him and looped my hand around his elbow.

He stilled at the touch before he cleared his throat. "Yes."

My eyes absorbed the details of the wardrobe. Beautiful rose blooms graced the center of the cornice, edging the top of the furniture. Then vining stems with little rosebuds trailed outward on each side. The leaves of the rose stems included lifelike details. All carved by hand by this man. This crafts-man.

It surprised me, as I released his arm, how the longing of my heart for years had been for a craftsman. I knew my sisters thought me odd. Honestly, I never understood it either. Not until that moment.

I grew up in a home where my mama was the perfect help-mate for my papa. Her spunky love of life drew him from his quiet contemplation. They were both gifted at training the horses. Papa managed the business side. Mama helped him by showing off the graceful horses' newly learned skills. Alone, they each had incredible strengths. Yet, together, their strengths built each other up and made them successful partners in their business.

Perhaps that notion worked its way into my heart over the years, leading to my longing for a craftsman. Maybe God made me the perfect helpmate for such a man. A man like Josiah. How I hoped he might be the one I'd been waiting for.

CHAPTER 7

JOSIAH

As Caty rested her hand on my arm, I relished her closeness. I watched her as she studied the details of the wardrobe. Suddenly, the desire to create something beautiful for her overwhelmed me. I had no time left to make her a gift. But oh, how I wanted to.

"Will it dry by morning?" she asked, breaking the silence.

"I think so."

Then the clock struck midnight, and she jumped.

"Oh, I promised Uncle Thomas I'd be home. I must hurry."

"Wait," I said as I touched her arm. "Let me escort you."

I retrieved both her coat and mine from the coat rack. Then I held hers as she slid her arms into the sleeves. I shrugged my coat on and wrapped a scarf around my neck before I offered her my arm.

We walked in silence to her uncle's home. Snow lightly fell in the quiet night. The gas streetlamps cast an ethereal glow over empty streets. I glanced at Caty. Her cheeks turned rosy from the cold. Her green eyes sparkled in the serene night. My heart grew ever closer to hers the more time I spent with her.

"This is it," she whispered.

As we stepped onto the porch, she faced me. I swallowed the lump in my throat as I stared into her lovely green eyes. My hands slid down her arms until I held her icy fingers. Then I tugged her ever so slightly toward me. She placed her arms around my middle as my hands settled at her waist. Then I leaned forward until her warm breath mingled with mine.

"May I kiss you?" The question burst from my mouth before the thought fully formed in my mind. My heart pounded against my chest as I waited for her answer.

Her eyes met my gaze. Then she took a deep breath, and the word left her lips in a whisper. "Yes."

Then I reached up and placed a hand on her neck as I closed the distance between us. My lips brushed across hers, softly at first. Tentatively. Wondering if she felt the same magnetic pull I did. Soon enough, she returned my kiss with her soft lips, chasing away all my doubts. I wrapped my arms around her, pressing her close. Despite the thickness of our coats, the warmth of her body sent my heart racing. She fit perfectly right there against me. My lips continued to taste hers, as sweet as those gingersnap cookies.

When I heard the latch of the door lift, I slowed the kiss. She released her hold on me as I slid my hands back down to her waist. I could stand there forever with her.

"I think I'm falling for you, Josiah Elliot," she whispered as she turned and ducked inside of her uncle's house.

"I know I'm falling for you, Caty Larson," I whispered into the night as I rested my hand on the closed door, trying to prolong the connection I felt with her. After a minute, I turned and headed back to my workshop as the snow fell faster.

Warm thoughts of kissing Caty kept me company as I completed the last order around two in the morning. I cleaned up the shop, locked the door, and headed home to fall into my bed dreaming of a blond-haired beauty with the biggest heart.

The next morning, I woke to the smell of bacon and whatever else Mama cooked over the stove. I hurriedly washed up and dressed for the day before I joined my family at the table.

"Good to see you, son," Papa said. "Your mother tells me you need some help to deliver a piece of furniture this morning."

I nodded as I swallowed a bite of food. "I have a few stops to make."

Mama smiled at me. "Did you finish everything?"

"Barely."

"Excellent. Then, after you complete your deliveries, we can enjoy Christmas Day as a family."

When we finished the meal, Papa and I met up with Drew and Wade Anderson at the workshop. Wade was only thirteen, so he managed the wagon, while Papa, Drew, and I lifted the wardrobe onto the back of it. We drove the wagon to Frank Murphy's large home. I wasn't sure if we'd have to carry the piece to its final destination. It relieved me to learn he had men lined up for that. Within minutes, the piece was unloaded. Frank paid me the balance due with a sizable tip.

"It's even finer than I hoped, Mr. Elliot. I'm certain Mrs. Murphy will adore it and tell all her friends where we purchased the piece."

"Thank you, sir."

We made two more stops for the other items I finished late last night. Then Drew and Wade took the wagon back to their father's livery, leaving Papa and me to walk alone.

"Your mother tells me Caty Larson has been spending a lot of time with you this week."

Heat burned my cheeks as I thought of our kiss last night. Or was it this morning? Regardless, it had been a delicious kiss, one that left me longing to see her again today.

"I had hoped to ride out to her place this afternoon, if it

wouldn't upset Mama. I… I'd like to spend some time with her."

What I really hoped was to ask her if she'd accept a courtship with me. But first, I needed to meet with her father to see if he'd bless it. I certainly hoped so.

"So, it's serious then?"

I nodded.

Papa squeezed my shoulder. "It's about time you found a good woman. Your mother and I have prayed for her for a long time."

"For Caty?" I asked, wondering how they knew before I did.

"I suppose so. Neither of us knew she was it."

When we returned home, Mama gathered us in the living room near the fireplace to exchange gifts. After I glanced at the clock a third time, she confronted me.

"Do you have some place to be?" Her annoyance was clearly evident.

I shook my head, deciding I would need to let go of the idea of seeing Caty on Christmas Day. Once we exchanged gifts, I asked Papa if we could talk privately. Our small house was not conducive to such a conversation, so we walked down to Anderson's Livery, where we stabled our horses.

"What's on your mind?" he asked.

"I'd like to court Caty," I said. "With the intention of marrying her early next year."

Papa's hand paused the brushing down his horse. He cleared his throat. "That's pretty fast, don't you think?"

"Maybe. I have been praying for the right woman for a while. I have no doubts Caty is that woman."

"You think she feels the same way?"

"Last night she told me she is falling for me."

Papa smiled. "Then you'll need to speak to Adam and Julia

for their blessing. You will need a place to live." He laughed. "Because I don't think you want to live with us."

My face heated. "No, sir."

His smile faded. "You should also speak to your mother. She'll want to hear how you feel about her."

"Do you think she would mind if I invite Caty and her family to Sunday supper tomorrow?"

"I think she'd like that."

We discussed plans for purchasing a house, how much it might cost, and then we prayed for wisdom and patience.

Once we returned home, I spoke at length with Mama. At first, she was concerned that I might move too fast. As I answered each of her questions, she changed her mind.

"Clearly, you've given the choice of a wife a great deal of thought, even before you met Caty. We would love to host her and her family for Sunday supper tomorrow."

I beamed, as I could hardly wait.

CHAPTER 8

CATY

WHEN WE ARRIVED at church on Sunday, Josiah met me at our wagon and helped me down. My heart fluttered as his smile warmed me from head to toe.

"Morning," he whispered. "You look lovely this morning."

My cheeks warmed.

"May I sit with you during the service?"

I smiled. "I'd like that."

Then he turned his attention to my parents. "My family would like to host yours for Sunday supper today, if you don't have plans already."

Papa slowly nodded as he glanced at Mama. Mama accepted the invitation before Josiah placed my hand on the crook of his arm. Then he led me into church.

"That was unexpected," I whispered to him.

"But welcome?"

"Most definitely."

"I have much to speak with you about and hope that you'll walk home with me after service."

I smiled. "I'd love to."

As soon as the service ended, Josiah helped me with my

coat. Then he suggested my parents and sisters follow his family home. He told them we'd be along shortly.

"Caty," he started once we were alone. "These last few days have been wonderful. I feel like I've gotten to know you well."

"I feel the same."

He smiled as he brushed some snow off a bench. As I sat, he took a seat next to me and angled to face me.

"This might sound strange." His eyes darted away. "I have been praying for a woman like you, Caty."

His eyes traveled back to me.

"The way you look at me makes me want to be a man worthy of you. And the way you admire the artistic touches of the work I do… I thought it was an impossible dream when I asked God for just that."

My breath caught. I removed the glove from my hand and reached up to touch his cheek.

"Josiah, it doesn't sound any stranger than my prayers that God would bring me a craftsman to marry."

I laughed for a few seconds.

"I always thought of craftsman when I thought of my future husband. Such an odd request, don't you think?"

He turned his lips to my hand and placed a kiss on my palm.

"Not so strange to me."

Then he pulled me close against him. "Is it possible, Caty, that we've prayed for each other all this time and not known it?"

"I think so."

"So, I have two more questions for you," he said. "First, if your parents bless it, may I court you?"

I nodded as I smiled.

"Second, if after a few months of courting you still find me an acceptable match, would you marry me?"

"How could I do anything else?"

He grinned and ran a finger down my face. "As much as I'd like to kiss you right now, we best go. Mama won't be pleased if we linger much longer."

"Just one kiss?" I asked.

Then he brushed his lips ever so gently across mine. Slowly, he stood and held his arm for me. We walked arm in arm to his home, me and my craftsman.

Supper seemed a little awkward at first. Our parents knew of each other, but had spent little time around each other. Not surprising, since Perry Quinn's job didn't involve purchasing horses. Most of my parents' connections were in that vein or family. Living far from town also limited our interactions.

My heart stuttered. How would a relationship work if I lived far away?

After supper, I helped Constance with the dishes so Rebecca, Josiah's mother, could socialize with my family. My sisters headed back to Constance's room, leaving only Josiah and our parents in the parlor.

When I joined them, he patted the spot on the couch next to him. Then he clasped my hand in his. Mama's eyebrow raised when he spoke.

"Mr. and Mrs. Larson." Josiah cleared his throat. "I wanted to ask for your permission to court Caty. These past few days, I've learned what a wonderful woman she is. She is compassionate and kind. She cares deeply for those around her. And she's been a tremendous help to me as I finished fulfilling orders in my workshop. I have a steady stream of business and am a hard worker—"

"Yes, we know. She's told us much about you," Papa said.

I couldn't read his expression and feared he might deny Josiah's request. I never considered that he might. It would crush me if he did.

As Papa reached for Mama's hand, he squeezed it. "It would

bring us great joy to allow you to court Caty."

I let out the breath I had been holding. Then I squeezed Josiah's hand. He turned and smiled at me. I was certain his happiness mirrored my own.

"Have you considered the logistics of that?" Papa asked.

My smile faded. When I glanced at Josiah, he swallowed hard.

"Do you think I could move in with Aunt Caroline? Or Aunt Bethie?" I asked. "That way, I'd be in town, which would give us more opportunities to get to know each other better."

Josiah turned to me. "Are you certain?"

I nodded. "I'll ask them before we head home today."

A smile tilted up one side of his mouth before he turned his attention back to my parents. "Would that be acceptable to you both?"

Papa turned to Mama. In their special way, they spoke without words to each other before Papa gave his consent.

"Though, Caty, I think you should take a job while you live with one of your aunts so you can contribute to their household."

"Yes, Papa."

I glanced up at Josiah and a hint of a smile graced his lips.

"And not at Josiah's shop," Mama added.

I nodded, confident that soon enough, Josiah and I would start our life together.

A short time later, my family stopped by Aunt Caroline's house. She insisted she and Thomas would be happy to have me and chaperone me. She even suggested that her dress-maker friend might need some help at her shop.

Everything seemed to fall into place. It was only a matter of time before my dreams would come true.

CHAPTER 9

JOSIAH

BY THE FIRST week of January, Caty and I fell into a routine. On Sundays, we spent the afternoon out at her parents' home, giving them the opportunity to know me. On Wednesdays, I dined with her at the Anderson's home. On Fridays, we dined with my parents. Occasionally, I took her out to dinner.

The afternoon of January seventh, I purchased a home for us much sooner than I expected. James Colter had commissioned me to furnish his new mansion. I completed a dining room table and chairs, which Caty helped me upholster under Mama's watchful eye. I also made a desk, several chairs for his parlor, bookcases for his library, and cabinets throughout the home. The sum I received more than covered my expenses with money left over to purchase our new home.

Caty and I picked the house together. Soon enough, I'd have it furnished and ready to offer her as a wedding present. I could hardly wait. I hoped we could marry by the middle of February.

After I dropped her off at the dress shop, I rounded the corner toward my workshop. The scent of smoke drifted in the air. My heart thrummed against my chest as I saw plumes billowing from the vicinity of my workshop. I walked, then jogged, then full out ran toward my business.

Firemen doused water from the water truck on my shop.

My stomach clenched, and bile rose in the back of my throat. Ash and charred wood littered the area where my shop once stood. The back room was unrecognizable. Flames sprung to life where my sample cabinets once sat before the firemen sprayed it with water. Another hot spot flickered near a display case.

Nothing remained.

My eyes burned, perhaps from the smoke in the air. I lost my source of income in a few hours. My dream of a life with Caty faded. I couldn't ask her to be my wife when I had nothing but a house.

"Josiah." One fireman I recognized from church jogged up to me. "I'm so sorry. The fire is almost out. You'll be able to see if there's anything salvageable soon."

The loss hit my gut hard. Everything I worked for was all gone. I had saved for years, slowly buying the tools of my trade. To replace it all… I couldn't fathom it.

As soon as the firemen allowed it, I started picking through the rubble. I started in the store's front with the least damage. A few jewelry boxes, figurines, and frames were salvageable with a little touch up. I set them in a pile to take… I supposed I'd take them home or to my new house. Or perhaps I should sell the house.

"We can store the salvageable items at the freight office," Papa said.

I looked around. There he stood, soot stained next to Mama and Constance. I did not realize they'd come.

"Josiah!" Caty's voice snagged my attention. Her eyes brimmed with unshed tears before she drew me into her arms. I held on tight for several minutes before she leaned back. She rested a hand on my cheek.

"We'll rebuild it. Or perhaps we can convert the parlor to a store for now and build a workshop out back."

"Caty." I whispered her name. "It will take years for me to replace my tools."

She grabbed my hand and led me to the workshop area. "Maybe some of them survived. Let's look."

I reached out to stop her from kneeling. "Please, don't ruin your dress."

"It's replaceable. Let's look together."

She kneeled anyway and dug through the piles of ash. Something metal caught my eye as I crouched next to her. I carefully wiped the ash from it. Then I opened the box. My carving tools miraculously survived inside the metal case. Though the handles discolored from the heat, they were still usable.

Caty turned her sweet smile toward me. "See. There may be more buried here."

We worked in silence, side by side, picking through the piles of burned wood and soot. The most expensive tools were beyond repair, but a few survived.

As the sun lowered in the sky on what should have been a happy day, I ran my hands through my hair. Then I stood and walked Caty back to her uncle's home. I faced her under the privacy of the porch.

"You should forget about me, Caty. It will take too long for me to rebuild to a point that I can provide for you."

"Don't say that. Don't give up. We'll find a way."

"It's not your problem to solve."

She frowned and propped her hands on her hips. "I love you. We want to marry, so that makes it my problem too."

"Don't you see? I'm trying to let you leave. We aren't tied to each other yet. There is time for you to find someone else."

Caty stepped closer to me and placed her hands on each of my cheeks. "I love you. You stubborn man. I will wait for you as long as it takes. Or we could marry anyway and figure it out together."

My eyes burned as I gazed into hers. She didn't understand how long it would take. I was trying to give her a reason to move on.

I brushed her hands away. Then I turned and walked down the street without so much as a parting word as I left my heart behind.

CHAPTER 10

CATY

"Aunt Caroline, he still won't talk to me," I said as I flopped down at the table after putting away the supper dishes. It had been a week since the fire.

My aunt poured us and Lily a cup of tea. Then she crossed her arms and tapped a finger on her temple. I'd heard the stories from Mama about my aunt's tick when she schemed. Hope flickered in my heart. Perhaps she had an idea that would help.

"We need to enlist the help of the Women's Aid Society to mobilize some volunteers to help him rebuild," she said. "Let's see if Rebecca is home."

I frowned. "Don't you think he'll be upset if I involve his mother?"

"You aren't enlisting her help. I am."

Aunt Caroline donned her coat. Lily and I followed as she led the way to Rebecca Quinn's home.

"Caroline!" Rebecca greeted her friend as she opened the door. Then she hugged me and Lily before she offered us tea. Constance joined us.

"He's not home," she said as she set a cup in front of me. "And Perry is traveling, so I'm glad you've come by."

My shoulders slumped. I had hoped to glimpse Josiah, if for nothing more than to remind him of my presence.

"We need to involve the Women's Aid Society," Aunt Caroline said. "Josiah should not figure this out on his own. We're a community and if the society isn't helping with this, then we're not living up to our mission."

"I am glad you brought that up," Rebecca said. "I have been trying to discern how to open the topic at our next meeting without sounding like I am looking for special treatment for my son."

"You leave that to me. I'll spread the word for a special session. The ladies will come up with a solution."

We shared some ideas about how we could help. Then, around eight o'clock, the door opened.

"Oh." Josiah's face brightened for a moment before he masked it.

"Josiah," I said as I stood to join him. The dark circles under his eyes revealed his exhaustion. I missed him so much.

"Caty." He hovered near the hallway to the bedrooms.

"Can we please talk?" I asked.

"I need to clean up and get some supper. I'm sorry." Then he dashed down the hall.

My eyes burned, and I donned my coat as my aunt and cousin waited for me. The tears fell as we walked home in silence. When we arrived home, I retired for the night, praying that God would provide a way to help restore Josiah's shop.

Two days later, I took a few hours off from the dress shop to attend the Women's Aid Society meeting. Aunt Caroline led the discussion.

"Ladies, as many of you know, one of our shopkeepers in town lost his business because of a fire. We must help him rebuild. He needs new tools and supplies and a new shop."

"I can meet with several of the railroad executives to request donations for the funds to rebuild," Mrs. Murphy said.

"I'll meet with the sawmill owner to organize the materials to rebuild the shop," another woman said.

"My husband will gather workers and supervise the construction," Millie Lancaster said.

By the end of the meeting, many women volunteered. They met all our needs. The construction of Josiah's new shop would begin on Friday.

I whispered a prayer of gratitude on my way back to work.

That afternoon, Josiah stopped by the dress shop. My heart warmed when I saw him. When he entered, he removed his hat.

"I hope I'm not too late," he said. "I have completed the keepsake box for your mother's birthday."

I smiled warmly. "Her birthday is today. We were going to celebrate on Sunday."

He let out a long breath. "Oh, good. Would you like me to drop it off at your uncle's house?"

"Do you have it with you? Can I see it?" I asked as excitement filled my soul.

He cleared his throat. "It's in a wagon outside with a few other deliveries."

I grabbed his hand and raced out the door. "Show me."

When he slid the box toward the edge of the wagon bed, my breath caught.

"Oh, Josiah! It's even better than I expected."

I ran my fingers over the beautiful carving of the horse on the top of the box. He used a darker stain on the graceful, galloping horse, which caused it to look almost as if it might run right off the box and come alive. As I lifted the lid, I smiled.

"It's perfect. Better than perfect."

When I dug through my reticule for the remaining balance I owed him, he placed his hand on mine. My pulse sped up.

"Keep your money."

"But I still owe you."

He snorted. "It's I who owe you, Caty."

Then he climbed up into the wagon seat and drove away.

Friday could not arrive soon enough, for my love needed a dose of humble pie to knock some sense back into him.

When Friday morning dawned, I put on a worn work dress, ready to help with the construction of Josiah's workshop. Papa and Mama met us at Aunt Caroline's and we walked to the site together. My jaw dropped when I took in the sight before me.

All my cousins from Colter Ranch set up work benches. Pails of nails and other building materials lined the street. Over thirty men gathered as Paul Lancaster assigned work. Papa, Uncle Will, and my cousins made quick work of framing the new building. A general store owner in town dropped off a new heating stove. Others brought supplies or physical labor.

I watched as Rebecca, Perry, Josiah, and Constance approached. Josiah's eyes grew wide. His jaw slackened. Perry said something to him and squeezed his shoulder before they joined in.

Rebecca came up next to me. "I think after today, he might change his mind about calling off things with you."

"I hope so," I whispered, for I yearned to marry Josiah Elliot and start our life together.

CHAPTER II

JOSIAH

WHEN I ARRIVED at the remains of my workshop, I could scarcely believe my eyes. Friends and family worked on rebuilding my business.

Papa leaned next to me and recited some verses from Psalms to me. "I lift up my eyes to the hills, from where does my help come? My help comes from the Lord, who made heaven and earth."

Then he squeezed my shoulder. "Shall we get to work?"

I nodded and followed him over to the framed structure.

"Oh, good. You're here," Paul Lancaster said. He showed me the plans and asked if I wanted to change them.

The workshop was larger than the old one, with more windows for light and ventilation. He suggested putting the new stove in the middle of the space between the workshop and store, so it would distribute heat more evenly across the store. I liked his ideas. With a few quick adjustments, we finalized the plans. Good thing too, as the volunteers finished the framing before lunch.

At lunch time, Caty found me and asked me to sit with her. I knew I owed her an apology, but the words stuck in my throat.

"So many people have donated items," she said as she sat across from me on a makeshift picnic table. "Someone donat-ed a new saw. Others brought by tools to replace ones you lost. The railway provided all the funds needed to con-struct the building."

The generosity of everyone humbled me.

Caty smiled and reached for my hand. "I think James Colter so appreciated the work you did at his home that he convinced the executives of the railway to contribute. He also told me he knows several other influential men who want to place orders for new furniture or cabinetry as soon as your shop is open again."

I bit off a chunk of sandwich as my emotions warred.

"I started a notebook with the orders, so we can prioritize which ones to work on first."

I cleared my throat. "We?"

She stood and rounded to the bench I sat on. Then she hugged my arm. "Yes, 'we.' Now you have no excuses to delay marrying me. Well, other than we still need to furnish our home."

"Caty." I angled to see her face. "I'm so sorry I pushed you away. I felt terrible that I could not provide for you. I didn't want you to waste time waiting for me when you could be happy with someone else."

"I could never be happy with someone else. My heart be-longs to you."

My pulse sputtered at her words.

"Forgive me for pushing you away."

"Already have."

My eyes searched hers. "Do you still want to marry me?"

"More than anything else in all the world."

I let out a shaky breath. Then I rested my forehead on hers.

"I don't deserve you. But I love you with all my heart. Thank you for everything you've done."

"Don't thank me, Josiah. Thank the Lord above. He is our help. He worked in the hearts of this wonderful community to provide all that we needed and wanted."

A loose strand of her hair whipped across her face in the cool breeze. I reached up and tucked it behind her ear. Then I lowered my lips to hers, confirming my deep love for my amazing woman.

———

As soon as my workshop opened again, the orders flooded in. Even though our wedding date was a few weeks out, Caty quit her job at the dress shop and started working with me. Her aunts or a cousin or my mother always made certain someone sufficiently chaperoned us.

"You're doing it again," I teased Caty.

She blew out a breath. "Doing what?"

"Biting your lower lip."

"Stretching the fabric is harder than it looks."

"Here, let me help." I brushed the sawdust from my hands and stood beside her. Then I gripped the edge of the fabric for the chair seat and pulled it taut. She tacked it down in a few places so it stayed taut.

"I think I've got it now."

"Mrs. Morrison will like the fabric you picked out," I said before I gave her a peck on the cheek, which drew Mama's attention. I grinned and returned to my lathe to finish fashioning the legs for a table.

"When I saw it, I thought it matched her fainting couch."

Caty had a gift for picking out the right finishing touches for our women clientele. On several jewelry boxes, she painted the carved petals of the roses pink or red. Then she painted the stems green, making each piece more beautiful. They became so popular, we barely kept them in stock. I loved the way she continued to surprise me with creative ideas like that.

When I finished the last table leg, I stretched before glancing at the clock. After I washed my hands, I ran them through my hair to shake loose any bits of sawdust that might cling to it. Then I held Caty's coat before I shrugged into my own.

She hugged my arm close as we leisurely walked to my parents' house.

"Only a few more weeks," she whispered.

"Mmm. I hope the time goes by fast. I can hardly wait to call you my wife."

"Me too."

I laughed. "I hope you won't call me wife."

She giggled. "You know what I meant."

Then she let out a contented sigh. "Have I told you about the starry night prayers me and my sisters prayed?"

"No, I don't think so."

"On my birthday last fall, we snuck out of the house to stargaze. We've done that a few times over the years. We shared our dreams about what our future husbands might be like. Then we prayed together about those dreams."

"And I supposed you asked for a handsome man?"

She laughed. "I did not. Though I'm glad God gave me one, anyway."

"Tell me, what did you ask for, then?"

"A craftsman. A man capable of making beautiful things out of nothing."

I laughed. "Really?"

She stopped walking and turned toward me. "Truly. When my sisters asked what I was talking about, I mentioned a man who loved woodworking."

My heart nearly burst to overflowing. She wanted a man just like me.

"Do you know what I asked for?" I asked.

"You prayed for a wife?"

"Of course. I needed all the help I could get."

She smiled as she slipped her arms around my neck. "What did you ask for?"

"A woman about yea tall," I said as I held my hand about her height.

She giggled. "What else?"

"A godly woman who would help me in my shop."

"Not a pretty woman?"

"No, though I suppose I should have."

Caty screwed up her face.

"But then I might not have found you, my beautiful almost wife."

Then she melted against me when my lips captured hers as I expressed the depth of my love for my wonderful Caty.

EPILOGUE

December 24, 1887

CATY

As I TURNED the shop sign to "closed," my husband pulled me into his arms and kissed me soundly.

"Thank you for all you did to keep us from being overwhelmed with last-minute orders this year. I really missed taking part in all the Christmastime activities last year."

"I know," I said as I rested my hand in the crook of his arm.

With each customer that came into the shop between Thanksgiving and the second week of December, I asked them if they had any orders for Christmas. I also let them know we would not accept new orders after the fifteenth. Our customers graciously worked with us.

The cold winter air and light snow added to the holiday feeling. Within minutes, we arrived at our home.

I smiled as Josiah helped me out of my coat. He rested his hand on my slightly extended belly.

"I will start on furniture for our little one next week," he said.

"That would be nice." I knew there was no hurry because our first child would not be born until the middle of March. It was very exciting to prepare the nursery.

When Josiah started kissing my neck, I leaned against him. I loved him so much and I had no doubts about his abiding love for me. We were a perfect match.

"Maybe we should skip the caroling tonight and cuddle up next to the fire," he suggested, his voice husky.

"Not a chance. I've been looking forward to this. So have you."

When he released me, I glanced over my shoulder to see his lower lip protruding.

"Don't pout. There will be plenty of time for cuddling after the caroling."

He laughed. "Fine. Will we stay up all night waiting to glimpse Santa and his reindeer?"

I snorted as I headed into the kitchen. He followed me. "We won't see him, you know."

"I know. I'm just practicing for next year when our son or daughter is around."

As I lifted the roast from the oven, Josiah set plates on the table. Everything smelled delicious. I grabbed some bread I baked this morning and sliced it. Then we sat down and enjoyed our Christmas Eve supper.

Once we finished washing and drying the dishes, Josiah and I changed into something nicer for the Christmas Eve service and caroling. When we arrived at church, my family greeted me warmly.

"I remember this time last year," Dory said to Josiah. "You were busy at the shop falling in love with my sister."

"And she was busy falling in love with you," Penny added. "Now look at the two of you. Happy as could be."

We slid into my family's pew before the service started. This year, the Women's Aid Society decorated the sanctuary with burgundy ribbons, mini pine wreaths, and even more candles than the previous year. A Christmas tree with popped corn strings and handmade ornaments graced the entrance. The smell of cinnamon and pine permeated the room. A few poinsettias lined the front of the altar. I took a deep breath and sighed contentedly as I sat next to my husband.

The children performed a reenactment of the night Christ was born after we sang several Christmas hymns. Then the pastor spoke a few words. We ended the service just like every year, with the congregation singing *Silent Night*.

As Josiah led me over to the refreshments table, I halted.

"Oh! I think the baby is kicking!"

I placed his hand on my belly. He grinned from ear to ear when he felt the kick. Such a sweet gift for us both on Christmas Eve. He kissed my cheek before he snagged three of my gingersnap cookies.

A few minutes later, Josiah helped bundle me up, and we joined our families and several others caroling. When the festive evening came to a close, we returned home.

Josiah built a fire in the fireplace. Then he brought me a footstool, and we sat on the couch staring into the flames. After several minutes, he stood.

"I can't stand it any longer."

He hurried upstairs. Then he brought down a wrapped gift.

"You must open this tonight. I have other gifts for you for tomorrow, but this one, I wanted to give to you on the one-year anniversary of our first kiss."

Josiah set the gift on my lap before he sat next to me again.

Slowly, I untied the ribbon. Then I slid the paper from the most elegant wooden box. I ran my hand over the carved image of a butterfly. So lifelike and beautiful. Tears burned my eyes as I opened the box. There rested the cookie tin I gave him last year.

As he placed his arm around me, he said, "I thought you might like your own keepsake box for us and our growing family. Though, I suspect this will be the first of many, because I plan to fill it with treasures for you."

I sniffed. "I love it. Thank you."

After he took the box from my hands, he set it on the floor before he pulled me into his arms. Then my craftsman kissed me senseless, and I enjoyed kissing him back, grateful God had answered my starry night prayer.

IN LOVE
WITH THE
RANCHER

*Let all bitterness and wrath and
anger and clamor and slander
be put away from you,
along with all malice.
Be kind to one another, tenderhearted,
forgiving one another,
as God in Christ forgave you.*

—*Ephesians 4:31–32*

CHAPTER I

Larson Stables
Near Prescott, Arizona Territory
February 14, 1893

PENNY

"DORY, I DON'T feel up to it," I said as I rolled over to face the wall.

Dory placed both hands on my shoulder and rocked me back and forth until I growled.

"Come on."

"He hasn't written. Not once since he moved," I said.

"So? Have you written to him?"

"No."

She continued rocking me back and forth. "Maybe you should. He is our cousin, after all."

"Stop!"

"Shh! You'll wake Mama and Papa."

I flopped onto my back and glared at my younger sister. Not that she could see me in the dark. When she tugged on my arm, I finally rose from the bed.

"Thank you," she whispered.

Dory shoved my coat toward me. "I miss Caty."

I sighed. I missed her, too. She could give me advice about Nathan. But with a five-year-old, a toddler, and another on the way, she was far too busy for her spinster sister.

After I donned my coat, I followed Dory out to the dock. We sat down, then leaned back and gazed at the stars overhead. Ever since Caty married on Valentine's Day, Dory and I decided we'd continue our stargazing tradition on that day.

The tears burned my eyes before Dory said a word.

"I miss him so much," I said, my voice thick with sorrow.

"Oh, I know, sis. But you really ought to write to him. He's probably thinking about you but is afraid to write."

I snorted. "Nathan Cahill isn't afraid of a single thing."

"Hmm. He might be afraid of ruining your friendship if he tells you how he feels."

"He can't feel much, considering he hasn't written at all. Aunt Mary says nothing to Mama about him pining for me. He moved away eight months ago and forgot all about me."

Dory sighed. "I'm sorry your dream of marrying Nathan Cahill seems unattainable."

I sniffed and pulled my coat tighter over my nightgown.

Once my emotions settled, I asked her what her dream was.

"To marry someone like Papa, still."

"It's good that your dream is not so specific," I said, as my disappointment with Nathan sliced through my heart. "That way, when you meet a man, if it doesn't work out, you won't be so crushed."

When I choked on the last word, I gave up trying to hold back my tears. I cried out all my feelings. And when I finish-ed, I resolved to forget all about Nathan Cahill and move on with my life.

CHAPTER 2

Cahill Ranch
Near Congress, Arizona Territory
June 2, 1893

NATHAN

AFTER A YEAR, I still thought about Penny. Her bright smile and sparkling blue eyes. That wild curly brown hair. I loved the way it bounced in the wind when she rode at a gallop.

A year ago, Papa, Mama, and I moved away from Colter Ranch and Larson Stables, leaving behind my cousins. Though I missed many of them, the one I missed the most was not even a cousin by blood. My mama's first husband was Penny's uncle. So Penny and I were cousins by tradition.

When I first developed romantic feelings for her, it seemed wrong. I grew up with her. She was nine months older than me. She had always been my closest friend, even though Deacon Colter and I were almost one month apart.

I smiled as I thought about her. Tomboy. Adventurous. She wasn't afraid of anything, not even breaking horses. I shook my head. Perhaps that added to my confusion when I noticed her maturing into a lovely young woman.

"Nathan!" Papa yelled to get my attention.

My gaze followed his pointing finger. I directed the stray calf back to the herd. I ought to stop daydreaming about Penny Larson and pay attention to my job.

It was no use. She'd been on my mind a lot. I missed her. I missed her friendship. What might have happened if I'd kissed her the last day I saw her—the day I moved away? I wanted to kiss her for a long time. On that day, I thought she might want me to.

No matter. I hadn't kissed her. Instead, I mumbled an awkward goodbye. As I rode out of her life, I convinced myself it was better if I let her go. She'd find someone else and marry. It was as it should be.

I sighed as we neared the corral. I slid off my horse and held his reins while I opened the corral gate. As soon as Papa and our cowhands directed the cattle into the pen, I closed the gate. Then I took my horse to the barn to care for him before I walked to our house.

"Nathan!" Mama called from the kitchen. "Is that you?"

When I entered the kitchen, she beamed. "I've just received the news. Cousin Penny is getting married."

I staggered backwards until I found a chair. All the air left my lungs. Not my Penny.

"Married?" I choked on the word.

"Yes, in three weeks. Aunt Julia wants to know if we'll come up for the wedding. I was thinking we could. I mean…"

The ringing in my ears drowned out whatever else Mama said. Married. Penny. And not to me.

For the first time in years, I knew what I really wanted. I wanted her as my wife. Not as my cousin. Not to marry some stupid stranger that didn't know her like I did. Me.

"Nathan? Did you hear me?" Mama asked as I backed away

from the table.

I waved my arm in the air as I fled from the room. I had to go. To Prescott. To Penny. I had to tell her how I really felt before it was too late, and she was gone for good.

I ran up the stairs to my room and started grabbing things. A shaving kit. Denim pants. A shirt. What else?

"Ahem." Papa's voice sounded behind me. "What's gotten into you?"

"I have to go see Penny."

He frowned as I pushed past him.

A firm hand clamped down on my shoulder. Then Papa steered me back into my bedroom until I sat on the edge of the bed.

"Explain yourself."

I tossed my hat on the bed and ran a hand through my hair. "She's about to make the biggest mistake of her life. I must stop her."

"Marriage? I doubt her parents would let her marry someone unworthy."

"You don't understand. It's a mistake. She can't marry some stupid stranger."

Mama slid past Papa and sat next to me on the bed.

"Why not?" she asked as she reached for my hand.

When I jumped to my feet, she gasped.

"Because I love her. She can't marry him because... Because she must marry me. We are destined to be together."

I turned my wild eyes on Papa first. Then Mama.

Papa's eyes shadowed as his mouth turned downward. "You may be too late, Nathan."

"It's not too late until she says her vows. There's still time. I must stop her."

Mama laid a hand on my arm. "Think about it, son. We've been gone for a year. Have you ever said anything to her about your feelings?"

I shook my head as my stomach tightened. "No. I should have. I'm so stupid."

Papa let out a long breath. "Take a deep breath. Stay the night. If you still feel the same in the morning, I'll drop you at the train station in Congress. You can tell Adam you're looking for two new horses for us. It won't be a lie. I was planning on making a trip up soon for that purpose. Now, you'll see to it instead."

Every muscle in my body coiled. I had to go. Waiting until morning seemed like too long.

"Sit," Mama said. "Let's pray for you. And for Penny."

I did as she asked, though I paid no attention to the prayer. I did not know how long it would take to get to her. No matter what it required, I must convince her she loved me.

The next morning, my mind did not waver. Just as Papa promised, he rode with me to the train station. I took my horse so I could ride out to Larson Stables as soon as I arrived in town.

As the train chugged slowly up the mountain, I considered my options. I had very little time to convince her not to marry someone else.

Ugh! If only I had kissed her. Or written to her. She would not have given up on me.

My mind churned as the train pulled into the Prescott station. Seconds seemed to tick by slowly as I waited to retrieve my horse. As soon as he was ready, I mounted him and pushed him for speed to Larson Stables.

At the top of the last hill, I slowed my horse and studied the scenery from my childhood home. Nothing had changed. The buildings looked the same. Aunt Hannah and cousin Ellie Mae hung out the laundry to dry. Uncle Adam and Aunt Julia worked with a horse in the corral. An odd sense of belonging washed over me. After a year, this place still felt home.

I nudged my horse down the lane to the barn, where I dismounted. Then I led him into the stable and searched for an empty stall. Once he settled, I turned around and stopped short.

There Penny stood, with her back turned to me, looking all gorgeous and wonderful. As she leaned over to brush a gray mare, her wild curls slipped over her shoulder. She felt like home, more so than the ranch itself.

What a stupid fool I was to leave her.

I cleared my throat before I said her name.

CHAPTER 3

PENNY

"PENNY."

The voice I pined over sounded behind me. Instantly, my heart raced faster than a galloping mare. Slowly, I forced myself to stand up straight. I took my sweet time as emotions washed over me. Anger. Disappointment. Heartache.

Then I faced Nathan Cahill.

Words jammed up in my throat at the sight of his handsome face. He'd changed over the past year. He looked older. More mature. More manly. My breathing shallowed when my eyes connected with his. They were full of regret. Sorrow.

"Nathan." His name came out as a squeak before I found my words. "What are you doing here?"

I stepped closer and propped one hand on my hip as I clung to the mare's reins with my other hand.

"Wait. Don't answer that."

I led the mare past him back to her stall. Then I hung up her tack before I stormed back out to the open grooming area. Nathan stood there leaning up against the wall with one leg crossed over the other, balancing his boot toe on the floor. His denim pants fit him to perfection, which caused my pulse to quicken.

"What are you doing here?" I asked as I frowned at him.

He crossed his arms over his chest and studied me. My cheeks blazed under his stormy gaze. I should not feel what I felt. Not toward him. I was engaged to be married to Greyson. In three weeks.

At length, he finally answered my question. "I am interested in buying two horses."

"And you didn't think *that* warranted a letter?"

"There was no time to write."

"Because you had a horse purchasing emergency?!" I let out a sigh of disgust.

"Penny?" Greyson's voice came from outside. "Is everything alright, honey?"

Nathan stood straighter and muttered, "Honey?"

I glared at him until Greyson entered the stable. Then I plastered on a charming smile as I looped my arm around my fiancé's waist.

"Look, Greyson. *Cousin* Nathan is here." My words came out with a sarcastic flair.

"Oh, hey. A pleasure to meet you," Greyson said as he smiled and offered Nathan his hand.

Nathan ever so slowly stretched out his arm and gripped Greyson's hand firmly, judging by the way Greyson flexed his fingers after Nathan let go.

"Greyson," Nathan grunted out the name.

I closed my eyes, mortified that my worst nightmare played out in front of me. Then I opened them again.

"Well, *cousin*, I'm sure Mama and Papa will be excited to see you."

Then I ran out of the stables towards the house. When I entered the house, I slammed the door shut.

Dory jumped from her place at the stove. "What's got you

in a fury?"

I growled. "Nathan is here."

Dory's green eyes widened and her mouth formed a large "O."

"I don't recall Mama or Papa saying he'd planned a trip."

I grabbed some plates from the cupboard and set them on the table while Dory put the finishing touches on the noonday meal.

"Because they didn't."

"You don't think he's here because he found out about your wedding?"

As I turned to face her, I scowled. "He's a little late."

Dory cleared her throat and softened her voice. "It's not too late until you say 'I do.'"

"Pen, what's wrong?" Greyson asked as he entered the house.

I whirled around to face Greyson, hoping he had not heard Dory's last comment.

With two steps, he stood in front of me. He took my hands in his as he arched an eyebrow. I took a deep breath and let it out slowly. Greyson was nothing like Nathan. He had soft brown eyes and jet-black hair. Nathan's violet eyes had always mesmerized me, and his sandy hair made my fingers itch to touch it. Greyson was only a few inches taller than me, unlike Nathan, who stood nearly seven inches over me.

My eyes darted to the corner of the room as heat warmed my face. In less than ten minutes, Nathan turned my entire world upside down, and I feared Greyson would read it in my eyes. It was so unfair. I promised to marry Greyson. I loved him, didn't I?

"Hey." Greyson placed his finger under my chin and lifted my face so he could look into my eyes. "Tell me what's got you so upset."

Dory cleared her throat. She looked at the door, where Nathan stood as still as a statue. Papa stood behind him and announced his presence. Then both Mama and Papa greeted him.

"I'll tell you later," I whispered to Greyson.

Once he held out a chair for me, I sat down. He took the chair beside me, while Nathan sat directly across from me next to Dory. I caught the glimmer of amusement in her eyes. The little skunk.

When Papa finished the prayer, he said, "This is a pleasant surprise."

I snorted. Pleasant? I didn't think so. Infuriating. Horrible timing.

Then I looked into Nathan's eyes and saw his heart before he masked it. A shiver traveled down my spine. *Get a hold of yourself, Penny.*

In three weeks, I'd be married. Mrs. Greyson Hastings. And there I was, feeling all soft and fluttery over another man. Another man who I spent the better part of five years longing for. And the last four months trying to erase from my soul.

Greyson leaned over, stirring me from my disturbing thoughts. "Are you feeling alright, Pen? You haven't touched your food."

Nathan muttered under his breath, "He knows 'Penny' is already a nickname for 'Penelope', doesn't he?"

I ignored Nathan's barb. Then I smiled reassuringly at Greyson and lied. "I'm fine."

As if to prove my point, I ate a bite of the delicious stew Dory made. Greyson appeared unconvinced but said nothing more.

Nathan finally answered Papa. "Papa sent me up to look at a few cattle horses. We've expanded and plan to hire two more men before the fall."

"Fall, huh?" I muttered. Not next week. No horse buying

emergency there.

He glanced at me with those darling violet eyes. "Yes, this fall."

When I glared at him, he turned his attention back to Papa. "It was a good time for me to leave."

Greyson spoke up. "I think Angel is ready. She's a strong cattle horse."

Mama nodded. "Excellent choice. Adam, what do you think about Titan?"

"Ahhh, I'm not sure. I think he could use a few more weeks before he's ready. Still more ornery than I'd like."

Greyson nodded. "Another two weeks and I think we can have him ready, if you're interested. We could always ship him down to your ranch. It's in Congress, right?"

As I swallowed a bite of stew, I wondered how Greyson knew that's where Nathan lived. Perhaps they'd discussed it after I stormed away.

"I was hoping Penny might ride with me as I observe the horses," Nathan said. "It'd give us a chance to catch up."

"Nathan and Penny were close friends growing up," Dory explained.

"You should go then," Greyson said.

"Absolutely not."

"Penny," Mama said, "It would be a big help to us if you could. Adam and I are working with the four-year-old Mr. Thompson is due to pick up on Monday."

"And I'm working with Mr. Adkins's skittish mare. The sooner I help her overcome her fears, the better. Mr. Adkins relies on her," Greyson said.

"Don't look at me," Dory said. "Not if you want your laundry cleaned and supper on the table tonight."

I let out an exasperated sigh. "Fine."

"Thanks, Pen." Greyson kissed my cheek. "Do you want me

to saddle Titan?"

I frowned. "I can do it."

"I can saddle him," Nathan said, "if I'm going to ride him."

"I don't think that's a good idea," Papa said. "He's used to Penny and still needs more work. I'd prefer you take Angel."

I stood and hurried to the barn without waiting for Nathan. The sooner we got started, the sooner we'd be done. And the sooner Nathan returned to Congress, the sooner I could move on with my life without him. That thought caused my heart to ache.

CHAPTER 4

NATHAN

MY HEART SANK when Penny flat out refused to go with me. I did not know how I could win her heart if she balked at spending time with me when Greyson suggested she go. Then a niggling of guilt punched my gut. I was there to take her away from him.

As soon as lunch finished, she leapt to her feet and rushed toward the barn. I stood and followed her at a reasonable pace. By the time I arrived in the barn, she finished brushing Titan. When she retrieved a blanket, she nodded toward a stall.

"Angel is two stalls down on the right."

Even though it had been a year since I'd lived there, all the grooming supplies and tack remained in the same place. I grabbed a brush and headed to Angel's stall. I led her to the alley. Then I brushed her down before I placed a blanket on her back. I set my saddle on her.

Titan snorted nearby. He shied away from Penny when she tried to place the saddle on his back. I frowned as I worried if she could handle him. She set the saddle down. Then she rubbed his face and spoke in soothing tones before she tried again. On the second attempt, she successfully positioned the saddle and cinched it.

A few minutes later, we led both horses out of the barn.

"Where were you going to take him?" Greyson asked as he held Titan's reins while Penny mounted.

"Through town toward the forest by Thumb Butte. We'll spend some time out there before we head home the back way. Once we spot the herd on the way back, we'll work with the cattle so Nathan can see how the horses handle it."

"Alright. Be safe."

When Penny leaned down to kiss his cheek, my hand tightened on the reins. Angel shifted, and I loosened my hold as I tried to calm myself.

"Ready?" she asked me.

I nodded.

She started Titan at a walk up the lane toward town. As I brought Angel beside them, I shot a quick prayer heavenward for the words to speak to Penny. Then I blew out a slow breath.

"How have you been?" I asked.

"If you'd written me, you would know."

The harsh words collided with my heart. I deserved them, as I had taken her friendship and her feelings for granted. We used to talk about everything. Now? I hoped our relationship was not beyond repair.

"I'm sorry."

She yanked back hard on Titan's reins, and he reared up, nearly unseating her. A lump lodged in my throat until his front hooves connected with solid ground again. Once she controlled him, she flashed angry blue eyes at me.

"You're sorry? Is that why you're really here? To apologize for... For... For leaving me and forgetting about me? Did I mean so little to you?"

Red rimmed her eyes as tears brimmed. My heart shattered.

"Penny—"

Without warning, she pointed Titan toward town and kicked him to a gallop. I pushed Angel to catch up. When I did, I angled Angel in her path, so she'd have to stop.

As Titan slowed, she came up next to me and wagged a finger in my face. Tears streamed down her cheeks. I longed to pull her into my arms and undo the damage I'd done.

"You almost kissed me, Nathan."

I glanced away as the guilt pressed down. I had almost kissed her the day before I moved.

We were in the stables. She wore a dress, not her usual flowing blouse and tan split skirt. She fashioned her hair into a coil at the base of her neck. That silky, enticing neck. When she smiled up at me, my blood pumped ferociously. Penny's beauty enthralled me. She had licked her pink lips, and I rested my hands on her waist, something I'd never done before then. I lowered my head and right when I almost tasted her lips, one of my cousins entered the stable. I stepped back and ran a hand through my hair. Then fled the scene without looking back. I would have never left if I did.

"I wish I had," I said. "I wish I told you how much you meant to me."

Penny lifted her chin and straightened her back. Then she pushed Titan into a trot. I followed her through town and up a trail into the forest surrounding Thumb Butte.

The safety of tall pine and juniper trees shaded us from the summer sun. She pulled Titan to a stop and dropped his reins. My stomach clenched. She knew better than to do that. Then she placed her face in her hands and sobbed.

I moved Angel next to Titan and grabbed the loose reins.

When she looked up, her eyes filled with regret. "I'm getting married. In three weeks."

"I know." I hoped not.

"To Greyson."

My throat worked as I reasoned through how to salvage our relationship. I wondered if laying my heart bare would convince her. Or perhaps I ought to beg her to forget about him and marry me instead. Clearly, as distraught as she was, she still felt something for me.

The sky darkened as she snatched the reins from my hand. A peal of thunder shook the ground as lightning shot across the sky. The smell of rain thickened the air.

Titan reared up, catching us both off guard. I watched in horror as Penny tumbled off his back, landing hard on the ground. He took off the way we came.

I dismounted my horse and ran to Penny. Her still form caused my heart to lodge in my throat. I felt her arms and legs, looking for injury. She made no sound. Then I lifted her head and felt the moist blood coating her hair.

Lord, please help her. Let her be alright.

Fat rain drops pelted the top of my hat as I cradled her in my arms. When she groaned, I let out a breath. She was still with me. As the rain fell harder, I looked around.

Angel disappeared. I forgot to tie her. It was me, Penny, and a monsoon storm in a forest. Not a safe place at all.

My eyes scanned the area. There was a rock overhang at the base of the butte a few yards away, which would provide cover from the rain and get us away from the trees. It was all that we had.

I lifted Penny in my arms and shuffled over to the alcove. Then I waited as the rain continued to pour from the sky. I shifted her closer to keep her from the worst of it. My legs were too long, and the rain soaked the lower half of my pants. As I held her close, my pulse raced. I loved her. She had to make it through so I could tell her. Then if she married Greyson anyway, I would not stand in her way.

When the rain finally let up, Penny still didn't stir. The sky grew dark, and I figured it stranded us until Penny woke up or someone found us. I carefully laid her on the ground. I left and gathered firewood. Once I made a fire ring, I got a blaze going. Thankfully, Papa drilled into my head to always keep some flint in my pocket, just in case.

As night fell, I laid down next to Penny and held her in my arms. I fell asleep to prayers for her safety and the hope for a second chance.

CHAPTER 5

PENNY

My head pounded as my eyes fluttered open. A fire glowed in front of me. I blinked. Strong arms held me close, the feel of them stirred something deep within me. That was where I belonged.

"Penny?"

I shot upright at the sound of Nathan's voice and immediately regretted it. The world spun, and I moaned. My stomach churned.

"Here, drink some water."

He held up a canteen to my lips. I sipped the water and my stomach settled.

"What happened?"

He exhaled. "Titan spooked when the thunder and lightning rolled in. He threw you before he ran off. Angel took off too."

"It's dark."

"Yup. I figure it's probably around midnight."

"We need to go."

"It's not safe to traipse through the woods at night. Neither of us are familiar with this area. We're too far from town," he said.

I turned to look at him. He looked terrible. Dark circles rested under his eyes. His disheveled hair matched his rumpled shirt. Mud coated the bottom of his boots. A streak of mud ran down one leg of his pants.

"At least I found a canteen. Don't know where it came from, but I filled it from runoff nearby. The water looked safe."

I snorted. "So you could have just poisoned me?"

He chuckled while I frowned. There was nothing funny about our situation.

"I would have poisoned myself first, Penny."

When I rubbed my temples, he pulled me against his chest. "Here, lean up against me."

My head hurt too much to argue.

Sometime later, I woke up again. His arms remained steadfast around me. I breathed deeply and caught the faint scent of his shaving soap. It was the manly smell I had always associated with Nathan. Oh, how I missed him.

The fire dimmed into golden embers as I sat up. His arms relaxed at his sides as I slipped away. My head pounded as I stood, so I gripped the rock wall until the worst of it passed. Then I found a secluded spot to relieve myself.

"Penny?"

The panic in Nathan's voice softened my heart.

"I'm right here," I replied as I stepped into the dim light from the fire.

He puffed his cheeks and blew out a breath. "For a second there, I thought you walked to town without me."

I snorted. "Not in the dark."

"Are you cold? Do you want me to find more firewood?"

As I slid down the rock to the ground, I told him I was fine.

"Why did you come here, Nathan, knowing I'm supposed to get married soon?"

He picked up a few dry pine needles from the ground and flicked them toward the fire.

"I needed to see for myself that you moved on from me."

Ire burned through me. "Moved on from you? What makes you think I ever had any interest?"

"That almost kiss."

My heart thrummed as he lifted his hand to cradle my cheek. I closed my eyes and savored his gentle touch, ignoring the accusing voice in my head. It seemed like a betrayal to Greyson to enjoy it so much.

"To see if you loved him."

My eyes flew open, and I pushed his hand away.

"You don't."

"I don't what?"

"Love him. You don't."

I crossed my arms over my chest. "Of course I do. I wouldn't marry him if I didn't."

"Penelope Larson, you know that is not even a little true."

As my eyebrows drew together, I growled. "What do you know about it?"

"I have eyes. I saw how you reacted to me. That was different than how you acted with him at lunch. In the barn. You don't love him."

"So, you came here to break up my relationship with Greyson? To destroy something good?"

"Yes, I did."

His honest admission jolted through me. It wasn't like Nathan, and it compounded my pain.

"You shouldn't settle for something good. You deserve so much more than that."

"But I love him." At least I thought I did.

Nathan drew me toward him. He ran his hands up my arms, leaving trails of fire behind.

"Does he make you feel like that?"

My heart raced as he placed a hand on the back of my neck and guided my face towards him.

"And when he's about to kiss you, does it feel like this?" He stopped until his lips were a breath from mine.

With his violet eyes dancing in the dim light, I could not look away. The air ignited between us. I leaned forward until my lips touched his and I closed my eyes. Then he wrapped his arms tightly around me as his lips demanded my heart. I surrendered to the thrilling kiss as I placed my hands behind his neck. When his hand lodged in my hair, I melted against him. His lips tore away from mine, trailing down my neck. His breath felt warm against my skin. I groaned and played with his soft hair. His hands roamed over my back, leaving lines of fire behind. I kissed him back with years of longing.

He abruptly halted the kiss and dropped his hold on me. Then he scooted away from me. My breath came in ragged bursts.

"No matter what lies you tell yourself, Penny, you still love me."

He stood and walked into the night, leaving me cold and confused.

CHAPTER 6

NATHAN

KISSING PENNY LIKE that made no sense. I must have left my common sense at home. It had to be the worst way to convince her she loved me and not Greyson.

When I pushed away, I launched to my feet. I needed some space away from her and that intoxicating kiss.

My bold words to her were nothing more than a hunch. The look in her eyes. The stiffness she exhibited with Greyson earlier in the day made me believe that not only did she miss me as much as I missed her, but she also loved me. Truly. I did not know it until that kiss.

After, well… I took a deep breath to slow my boiling blood. I would not allow her to marry anyone but me.

I ran a hand through my hair. Except I couldn't force her to marry me. I wouldn't want to.

The only thing to do was tell her the truth. Confess everything and then pray it would be enough for her to choose me.

After I walked back to the fire, I sat opposite her to avoid pulling her into my arms again.

"Penny, I'm not sure where to start, so here it goes."

She looked at me as she leaned against the rock.

"First, you have been my closest friend our entire lives. That should have been the reason I wrote to you. Or for you to write to me when I moved."

When she parted her lips, I held up my hand.

"But neither of us did."

I let out a long breath before I continued.

"The year we turned seventeen, I developed other feelings for you. I didn't know what to do with my feelings. You were my best friend and my cousin. It seemed wrong to suddenly notice your lovely figure or to desire to hold your hand. I spent several years trying to avoid the sparks I felt around you."

"Nathan, there was nothing wrong with you having those feelings. We aren't related by blood."

"I know that now. I just didn't understand it then. Maybe I was afraid of what our family thought. I don't know. All I know is that fear kept me from telling you or acting on those feelings."

As I gathered the courage for my next words, I rubbed my hands on my outstretched legs. Her eyes locked on mine. I had to press on.

"At some point, I realized I was attracted to you. I thought I might love you. As much as I wanted to be brave, I wasn't. I feared losing my best friend."

"So you left?" she asked.

"I left without telling you how I felt. The first weeks were pure torture. I'd see something at our new ranch and want to hurry home to tell you about it, only to remember that you weren't there. The weeks turned into months. I thought about you every day. And every night, I resolved to forget about you."

I cleared my throat.

"Then Mama read your mother's letter. You were getting married. I knew that I had wasted time. You can't marry some stranger. I want you to marry me because I have loved you for as long as I can remember. We are destined to be together."

Penny looked away. A tear slid down her cheek. My heart ached as I wanted to rush to her side and hold her. I wanted to kiss away her pain.

When she turned her gaze back to me, she let out a shaky breath.

"Destiny. You don't know how true that is."

Her words slammed against my heart. Maybe she would forgive me.

"Every year, my sisters and I snuck out of the house to gaze at the stars and share our dreams. When Caty still lived at home, we did that on her birthday. Once she married, Dory and I continued the tradition on Valentine's Day."

She lowered her head and fidgeted with the edge of her split skirt leg. When she raised her head, she said, "My only dream was to marry you, Nathan Cahill. For years, that was my greatest desire."

A shadow fell across her face. "Until this year. This year, I let you go. You left me without a single word."

"You broke my heart, so I moved on. When I met Greyson, he treated me well. He spent time with me. He makes me laugh. And he loves me very much."

I bit my cheek to keep from snorting.

"You're missing one very important point," I said.

"I promised to marry him."

"But you don't love him."

"And you hurt me. I'm not sure I can forgive you."

Her words sliced through my heart. *Lord, help her forgive me. Help her stop and think before she makes us both miserable.*

The sound of something crunching on the forest floor behind me drew my attention. I turned to see Angel walking toward us. As soon as the sky lightened, we rode double back to

Prescott.

We stopped by the doctor to have her head wound checked out. He said it was just a scratch. She probably had a concussion but would be back to normal soon.

When I mounted the horse behind her, I let her have the reins. I kept my hands on my knees, even though I longed to hold her in my arms.

As we started down the lane to Larson Stables, a man ran toward us. He met us halfway.

"Penny!" Greyson sounded worried as he reached up and helped Penny off the horse before he wrapped her in a tight embrace.

I lowered my head and continued on to the barn as numbness overtook me.

CHAPTER 7

PENNY

"Penny!"

Greyson placed his hands on my waist and lifted me from the horse. Then he engulfed me in a warm embrace. A lukewarm embrace that did not cause my heart to flutter. No shivers or tingles. Nothing like when Nathan held me.

He leaned back and stared into my eyes. When I failed to hold his gaze, he guided my head to rest against his chest. I watched as Nathan dismounted his horse outside of the barn. His shoulders slumped as he walked into the building. My heart bled.

"When they found Titan, we were worried. No one had seen you."

Greyson held me away from him and kissed my forehead. Though comforting, the kiss invoked no powerful feelings inside of me.

I pulled away from him as tears rolled down my cheeks. "I need to go lie down."

Then I raced towards the house and into my bedroom, where I fell onto my bed and sobbed. I heard the door creak open.

"Penny?" Dory called my name.

"Close the door." My voice sounded muffled in my pillow.

"What happened?"

Then I told her everything that happened with the horses, my head injury, and then I blurted out what weighed on my heart.

"He kissed me, Dory. Nathan kissed me."

The tears streamed down my face. My sister laid on her stomach next to me. Her green eyes searched mine.

"And you still love him."

It wasn't a question. I nodded, unable to deny it any longer.

"What do I do?"

Dory rolled onto her back. Her chest rose and fell with a heavy sigh. "You must choose. Greyson or Nathan."

"But I promised Greyson."

"You aren't married yet. I know it will hurt him, but if you don't love him or if you love Nathan more, you can't marry Greyson. It wouldn't be fair to him."

"I... I don't know what I want."

Dory sat up. "You need to figure it out. Nathan will head home soon. Your wedding is a few weeks away."

Then she stood and left the room.

I kicked off my boots and changed into a clean work dress. Then I fell back on my bed.

Greyson was a good man. Everything Papa wanted in a son-in-law. A horse trainer as good, or even better than Papa. The two men discussed the possibility of Greyson becoming a partner and eventually inheriting Larson Stables. I knew it was Greyson's dream. A dream that would not come true if I didn't marry him.

I frowned. I should not marry him for that reason.

Did I love Greyson? My stomach clenched tight. Before Nathan showed up on my doorstep, I thought I did. I enjoyed

Greyson's kisses. He was a godly man. Very similar to Papa.

The thought pierced my heart like a flaming arrow, burning away the lies I had allowed myself to believe. That was Dory's dream, not mine. She wanted a man just like Papa. My dream had always been Nathan, a man barely like Papa. A rancher. A funny, charming man who made me smile when I thought of him. My best friend since we were children. He knew me better than anyone. Maybe better than my sisters or my parents.

I allowed myself to imagine a life with Nathan. We'd live on his ranch in Congress. I'd be a rancher's wife, not a horse trainer's wife. If he kissed me like he did last night... We'd share a fiery passion. Try as I might, I couldn't picture anything as thrilling with Greyson.

Mama knocked softly on the door. "Supper is ready."

"Just a minute."

After I stood, I washed my face. Then I joined the family for the meal and noticed one person was missing.

"Where's Nathan?" I asked.

"He's dining with his other cousins tonight at Sam's house."

Greyson took my hand under the table and squeezed it. "Did you rest well?"

I nodded as my emotions tried to pull me under again. I took a swig of water.

"Did Nathan like the horses?" Dory asked.

"I'll take him out to the herd with them tomorrow," Papa said. "I think we need to keep Titan for another month to six weeks before he'll be ready. After he threw Penny, I'd hate to think he'd throw someone else during a storm."

"I can take him out with the herd," I volunteered.

"Are you sure?" Papa asked. "Will you feel up to it?"

"I think so."

Papa's eyes held mine for a long moment. My cheeks flushed under the intensity, and I wondered if he sensed the turmoil in my heart. He always seemed to read me.

"If you don't feel up to it in the morning, let me know."

I nodded.

After supper, I headed out to the barn. It had been a few days since I rode Cupcake. I entered her stall and ran a hand down her white blaze.

"Wanna go for a ride?"

When she nudged my arm, I placed the bridle on and led her from the stall. The motion of brushing down her tawny coat soothed my tumultuous feelings. I knew I must break off my engagement. It was the right thing to do after kissing another man. Even though Nathan started that kiss, I kissed him back with abandon. That alone was enough to release Greyson.

After I saddled Cupcake, I led her outside. Then I climbed onto her back. I nudged her toward the higher trail around the lake at a walk. Once I arrived at the highest point, I stopped and looked over the valley below. Colter Ranch and Larson Stables was the only home I'd ever known for twenty-three years. Never far from cattle, horses, cousins, and grandparents. I sighed. Life with Greyson would keep me there.

A life with Nathan would mean leaving this beautiful place and my parents, sisters, and extended family. I'd never been further than Prescott. All I knew about Congress came from Aunt Mary's letters. Flat prairie land nestled in the massive valley between two mountain ranges. Cattle land. From what Aunt Mary said, the town of Congress was significantly smaller than Prescott and more primitive, what-ever that meant.

Did letting Greyson go mean that I had to choose Nathan? Or should I wait and let Nathan go home without me?

Lord, I don't know what to do. Please show me what way to go.

The sound of a horse behind me drew my attention.

"Hey."

I swallowed hard and waited for him to continue.

CHAPTER 8

NATHAN

WHEN I SPOTTED Penny riding up the high trail overlooking the lake, I hurried to the barn and saddled my horse. I kicked him into a trot, hoping to catch her before she moved on from our spot.

I slowed my horse as I neared. She seemed lost in thought, so I studied her for a few minutes. How many times had we ridden up here? More than I could count.

"Hey," I said at last.

Penny turned in her saddle. Her downcast eyes and slumped shoulders did not inspire my confidence. Gone was her bright smile or the excitement she used to show when I met her here. Perhaps I had waited too long to tell her my feelings.

I cleared my throat. "How are you feeling?"

"Confused. Hurt. Lost."

I might still have a chance. Hope grew, even though it seemed wrong to be glad she felt confused.

"Do you remember our first time here?" I asked.

She let out a long breath and turned her gaze toward the lake. "Of course."

I smiled. "You had a fight with your sister. I think it was

Caty, over which one of you would help with laundry and who would help your papa."

"I ended up with laundry duty."

"Do you remember what I told you?"

She laughed. "Yup. Make it the last time I was told which chore I'd have to do."

"If I recall, after that day, you headed to the barn to muck stalls before anyone could tell you otherwise."

"It was good advice," she said. "I spent most days helping with the horses. Even the dirty tasks, like mucking the stalls. Once Papa saw what a hard worker I was, he advocated for me to work with the horses."

I nudged my horse beside her and looked out over the lake.

"I remember when you were supposed to go on your first elk hunt with your brother and papa. You sprained your ankle the day before."

I snorted. "I was really upset about that."

"And I cheered you up."

"Brought me some of Aunt Hannah's famous cherry pie, if I recall."

She laughed. "Not some. The whole thing. I stole it from her pie safe and everything."

"It worked. I forgot all about my disappointment, especially with you getting an earful for your thievery."

"And you went with them a few weeks later."

She sighed. "We have a long history, don't we?"

I nodded. "Would you really give that up? Would you marry a man you've only known for what, a few months?"

"Nathan—"

"If you tell me you're truly in love with him and I don't know what I'm talking about, then I'll head home tomorrow afternoon." As hard as it would be, I would leave if she asked me to.

The sun's heat let up as it lowered toward the horizon. Several cowboys rode in from the pastures and headed to the bunkhouse. Lights flickered on at my cousin Sam's house. I missed the scenic beauty of the place.

But I missed Penny even more. The last year without her left me feeling utterly empty. All the things I usually shared with her, I kept to myself. My life was not a grand adventure. I was a rancher, and my problems were ranching problems. It didn't matter. We'd always shared everything with each other. For the rest of my life, I wanted everything to include my heart.

"Tomorrow, I'll ride out with you to the herd," Penny said, apparently ignoring my statement. "We'll take Angel, and I think Papa has another horse for you to try."

Then she squeezed Cupcake's sides and raced down the path, taking my heart with her. I prayed God would make a way. I'd wanted nothing more.

———

PENNY

ALL NIGHT I tossed and turned, remembering many conversations from that mountain top. Like the evening when Nathan learned that his mother's first husband had been abusive. His anger and confusion took hours to calm. There was nothing he could have done about it. It happened long before he'd been born. The pain he felt on his mother's behalf showed how much he loved her. I listened and encouraged him through it all.

That was the man Nathan was. Compassionate to a fault. On the outside, he projected confidence and calmness. On the inside, he cared for his family and for injustice in the world. He wanted to be a man of action, no matter what.

Reality crashed down on me. As a man of action, he hopped a train and came to me the moment he learned he would lose me forever. My eyes burned. If only he'd acted sooner. Perhaps he could have saved himself, me, and Greyson so much pain.

Now I had to face Greyson and crush his heart. It sickened me, but it must be done. I did not love him, not the love I felt for Nathan. I knew my relationship with Greyson was over.

For the first time since Nathan showed up, I kneeled by my bedside and I prayed for wisdom. To let Greyson down gently but firmly. I prayed for clarity about the future.

After climbing back into bed, I slept for a few hours. My day of reckoning would dawn soon.

CHAPTER 9

PENNY

THE NEXT MORNING, I rose early. I tied my unruly curly hair back with a ribbon after I donned a cotton blouse and my split skirt. I plopped my tan hat down on my head as I hurried from the house before breakfast.

When I entered the stables, I took a deep breath. The sweet scent of hay filled my lungs. Horses shifted in their stalls, crunching hay under their hooves. The soft sound of footsteps behind me drew my attention. I turned to face the man I'd promised to marry.

As his eyes locked on mine, I let him see the distance there.

"What's happened between us, Penny? Did I do something wrong? Did I drive you away?"

Greyson's questions brought overwhelming guilt. He deserved the truth.

"You did nothing wrong," I said as I leaned back against the stable wall. "I should have told you about Nathan. About the dreams of my heart."

He frowned and crossed his arms over his chest.

"For…" I nearly choked on the next words as I thought about how much they would hurt him. "Six years I dreamed

Nathan would one day marry me. I loved him. I still love him."

Greyson's jaw twitched. His frown turned darker and his eyes smoldered.

"I'm sorry I wasn't honest with you. I thought I could forget about him. Never see him again. It had been eight months since he'd left by the time I met you."

When I reached out to touch his arm, he backed away. I swallowed hard as I squared my shoulders.

"You are a good man, Greyson. So much like my father. Godly. Kind. You made me feel special and wanted."

He dropped his arms to his side. "I still want you, Penny. I thought you loved me."

The hurt in his voice threatened to break my resolve.

"So did I. All I can say is that I'm terribly sorry, but I can't marry you. Nathan is wrapped up in my heart. It's not fair to you."

Moisture gathered in his eyes. *Lord, forgive me for denying my actual feelings and destroying this dear man.*

He set his jaw and pushed past me down the row of stalls until he reached Titan's stall. Then he led the majestic stallion toward the grooming area without a word. It was probably for the best. I had nothing else to say that would not heap more pain on his open wound.

Once I grabbed the bucket of oats, I fed the horses before I returned to the house for breakfast, feeling like a wicked betrayer.

When I closed the door, I exhaled. Then I took my seat at the table. Dory and Mama set the meal out.

"Where's Greyson?" Dory asked.

"I… I don't think he'll join us this morning," I said before I bowed my head, hoping Papa would pray soon.

A tear slipped down my cheek. It hurt, even though it was the right thing to do. Until a few days ago, I planned to spend the rest of my life with Greyson. We had shared dreams together.

"Amen," Mama said.

As I lifted my eyes, a frown creased her brow. "Penny—"

"Greyson and I will not be getting married." The matter-of-fact words felt cold and unloving.

"What happened?" Papa asked as he straightened in his chair.

I glanced away, relieved that Nathan had not joined us for the meal.

"Nathan did," Dory said.

My gazed dropped to my oatmeal as shame washed over me.

Papa cleared his throat. "What did Nathan do?"

"Love me," I whispered. I raised my head and locked eyes with my father. "I've loved him for years. He came here to tell me he loves me."

Papa's mouth formed a thin line as he set his spoon down. His eyes searched mine. Slowly, he lifted his coffee mug and took a swig. Papa wasn't prone to anger, so I couldn't tell if he was angry or disappointed. Either way, my heart ached.

Mama's brow crinkled. "Years? You never said. I did not know."

"Neither did I," Papa said. "If I did, I would not have blessed Greyson's proposal. Nor would I have treated him like the son-in-law I hoped he'd become."

I bowed my head as my shoulders slouched. My denial hurt a lot more people besides Greyson than I expected. The disappointment written all over my parents' faces made my stomach churn. I pushed back from the table as my eyes burned.

"I need to go. I promised to take Nathan to the herd this morning."

As my hand turned the doorknob, Mama called out behind me, "Have him ride Commodore."

I gave a sharp nod before I hurried out the door. I swiped away the tears that came. Greyson sped by without a wave. I did not know how hurt Papa would be. Now that I knew, I almost wished I could start the morning over and choose differently.

Not that I would have. I hoped pursuing Nathan was worth all this. Me turning my life and my family's upside down. There was no going back now.

As I walked toward the stables, I heard Dory call my name. She scurried up next to me.

"Are you alright? I know that must have been hard."

I sniffed, and my voice cracked when I spoke. "It was."

She snagged my arm and pulled me into a hug. My sister held me tight as I wept on her shoulder.

"Do you think Papa will ever forgive me?"

"Hush now. He would prefer you marry the right man. I think he was just surprised. Things will work out in the end."

I sighed. I hoped Dory was right. As I released her, I found my handkerchief and wiped my eyes.

"I better go. Nathan is probably waiting for me by now."

After Dory squeezed my hand, I walked the rest of the way to the barn.

When I entered the stables, I retrieved and readied Commodore. I lugged Nathan's saddle over to the horse and slung it onto the blanket on his back. He was a beautiful chestnut gelding. Perfect cattle horse. I thought my cousin Sam considered purchasing him, but I guess not.

Then I readied Angel and led both horses out near the corral. Nathan stood leaning against the railing. He smiled when he saw me. I gave him a tentative smile. Perhaps I made the right decision.

CHAPTER 10

NATHAN

THE NEXT MORNING, I met Penny at the corral. Her eyes rimmed with red. They darted away before I could study her longer. My pulse sped up. I hoped she did not decide to reject me in favor of Greyson.

She handed me the reins for a chestnut gelding. "This is Commodore. He's much more settled than Titan. He's a good ranch horse."

I eased into the saddle and followed Penny out to the herd. Once we neared the herd, she waved to the foreman to let him know we were evaluating the horses's interaction with the herd.

As Penny expertly cut a few head from the herd, I watched her and the horse. Her beautiful curls bounced as her body moved. The horse responded to her lead and her sharp shifts in direction. The horse performed admirably. She was truly a cowgirl, the perfect match for a rancher.

When she finished the task, she rode up next to me.

"Let's see what you've got, cowboy," she said breathlessly. Her blue eyes sparkled with challenge.

I touched my fingers to the brim of my hat. Then I squeezed Commodore's sides, and he shot off toward the herd. I found the calf I wanted to cut. Then we rode toward it. Commodore responded to my commands to move forward, block, and cut the calf. He was an excellent cattle horse. Papa would like him.

"Not bad," Penny said.

When I stopped next to her, I pointed my horse in the opposite direction of hers so I could get closer. We needed to talk.

"We'll take both Angel and Commodore, if that's alright."

"I think Papa will agree to that."

I cleared my throat as I rested my hand on the horn of my saddle. "What happened this morning?"

Her eyes darted away from me, and her mouth turned down. "I broke off my engagement with Greyson."

My pulse raced as I reached over to touch her hand. She looked at me as tears pooled in the corner of her eyes.

"Papa is upset with me. He was going to name Greyson his heir to inherit Larson Stables."

I straightened in my saddle.

"It's up in the air. All because of me." She sniffed and withdrew her hand.

"I… I don't know if I'm ready to pursue something permanent with you. It seems wrong to run away with another man in the same day."

My throat constricted. "What are you saying?"

"I don't know what I'm saying."

She kicked Angel into a gallop and headed back to the barn. I followed as Commodore tore up the distance between us. No way would I let her leave it at that. I needed to know if there was hope for us.

When Penny dismounted, she led Angel into the stable. After I dismounted, I grabbed the reins from her and tied both horses in the grooming area.

Then I took Penny's hands in mine. Tears spilled over, running down her cheeks. I pulled her into my arms and rubbed a hand over her back. Her arms wrapped around my middle as her shoulders shook. When she lifted her head, I wiped her tears away with my thumb. Then I brushed those lovely curls back from her face. As I breathed in, her hair smelled like apples and flowers, stirring my desire. My fingers slowly slid behind her ear and down her soft neck. I cradled her face with my hands. My eyes searched hers as her hands inched up my chest until they rested behind my neck. Her body rested against mine as I slowly lowered my head. She reached up and her lips met mine. The gentle kiss heated as I ran my hands down her back and pressed her hard against me. I explored her back before my fingers anchored in her silky curls. My heart pounded as she played with the hair at my nape. Love for her flowed through my entire being. I wanted to marry her and spend every day of my life with her by my side. Any other outcome pained me.

Slowly, she eased away from me. Her lips were plump and red as they stretched into a gentle smile. My fingers intertwined with hers. As she stepped back, our fingers remained connected.

I gave her a saucy smile. "That was some kiss, Penelope."

Her breath came out in a shaky *whoosh*. "Uh, hmm."

As she straightened her shoulders, I released her hand. "Let me tell Papa you'll take the horses."

When she walked away and reached out to the stable wall to steady herself, I grinned. Just maybe, that kiss convinced her we were a perfect match.

CHAPTER 11

PENNY

Nathan's kiss left me feeling unstable and cherished all at the same time. Warmth spread through my middle. There was no untangling my heart from his now. Not after that kiss. I wondered where we'd go from there.

I shook my head, hoping to clear the fog. Papa and Greyson worked with a horse in the corral.

"Papa!"

When he saw me, he let Greyson take over. Then he walked with me into his office in the barn. I sat across from his desk.

"Nathan wants both Angel and Commodore."

"That's good news."

When I stood to leave, Papa stopped me.

"Do you love him?"

My heart raced as I studied my father. His green eyes clouded as he leaned forward. His lips pressed into a firm line. Not an encouraging sign.

"Yes, I do."

Then he ran a hand through the graying edges of his golden hair as he expelled a loud breath.

"Do you want to marry him?"

"If you'll give your blessing and if he asks."

Papa snorted. "Oh, he'll ask. A man doesn't upend his life and the lives around him if he doesn't have marrying intentions."

For a moment, I wondered if Papa might refuse his blessing. I desperately wanted to honor both of my parents, but I wasn't sure I could if they forbade me to marry Nathan.

"When you leave in a few minutes, I'm going to speak with him. I'm going to ask him to take the horses and go home without you—"

"But—"

He held up a hand. "Hear me out."

I lowered my head slightly in deference.

"I'm sure his family will come up for the Cowboy Tournament on July fourth. If you and he still desire to marry, and if I can convince your mother of all this, then I will give my blessing. But not a day before then."

My shoulders slumped. I wanted to go with Nathan now. Not to wait a month.

"I think it's important for the two of you to pray over this. Clearly, you both have strong feelings for each other. You need to be positive this is God's plan for your life and not just infatuation."

I frowned. I'd known Nathan all my life. My love for him had grown over the years. It bothered me Papa didn't seem to understand that.

"You may write to each other. In fact, I'd encourage you to. But you also need to pray. Is that understood?"

"Yes, sir."

———

NATHAN

WHEN UNCLE ADAM asked me to take a seat in his office, my throat tightened. His stoic expression sent chills down my spine. I braced myself for an unpleasant conversation.

"I'm disappointed in you, Nathan."

My jaw tightened at the sting of his words.

"You have not done right by me or my family. Coming here with an ulterior motive. Not coming to me first regarding my daughter. We could have avoided a lot of tension by simply talking over things."

Uncle Adam cleared his throat. "You've also terribly wronged my business partner, Greyson Hastings, and you've caused me to retract the offer of Larson Stables as an inheritance to him."

When he paused for a breath, I quickly interjected. "I'm sorry. That was not my intention. I only thought about losing Penny forever. It broke my soul to think of it."

My uncle's face softened for a moment. "Love will do that to a man. Make him foolish and twisted inside out. That said, I have a few concerns."

I swallowed hard, wondering what those concerns might be.

"First, it does not speak well of you that you never wrote to Penny when your family moved away. When you return to your ranch tomorrow, how do I know you won't do the same thing?"

Regret churned my stomach. He was sending me home. "I promise I will write to her, though... I'd much rather take her with me, as my wife."

"Absolutely not. You need to repair trust with this family. Is your family coming for the Cowboy Tournament?"

"Of course."

"Then we can discuss Penny's potential future with you then."

I relaxed my fisted hand. Perhaps there was hope, after all.

"In the meantime, tomorrow you will return to your ranch. In the weeks between now and the tournament, I expect to see you both exchange a few letters, ones that might show you've prayed over this relationship and planned to provide a home for her. Not just the sweet sentiments of the heart. I need to be confident I can trust my daughter's well-being to you."

"I understand. And I am truly sorry for the trouble I've caused. My father tried to warn me not to be hasty."

"Wise man."

CHAPTER 12

NATHAN

THE NEXT MORNING, Penny and Uncle Adam rode with me to the train station. As much as I desired Penny to come home as my wife, I knew I must honor Uncle Adam's request. He asked me to pray, for goodness's sake. Besides, I would only be gone for three weeks. I had waited years to tell Penny how I felt. This time, we would handle it better.

After we loaded the horses on the stock car, I whispered my goodbyes to Penny. Since her father kept watch, I gave her a chaste kiss on the cheek.

"I'll see you in a few weeks."

"You better write, Nathan."

I smiled. Little did she know Dory agreed to place my first letter on her pillow. It waited for her at home.

"I will."

She let out a long breath before she thrust an envelope at me. "Here."

I quirked an eyebrow.

"I couldn't help myself. I wrote to you last night. You can read it on the train."

"I love you, Penny," I whispered.

The train whistle blew, cutting off further conversation. She squeezed my hand before I turned and boarded the train. As the train left the station, Penny waved to me from the platform.

As soon as we were underway, I opened the envelope and unfolded the letter.

Dearest Nathan,

Where to start? First, I love you still. Though Papa's request chafed, I see the wisdom in it. I will pray for you, me, and God's direction in our relationship while we are apart.

I am glad you finally came to your senses and kept me from marrying the wrong man. I will also pray Greyson will forgive both you and me for the pain we caused him. It must have hurt him deeply.

Alright, it's time to take you to the station. Know that my heart goes with you.

All my love,

Penny

I smiled for the rest of the ride home.

When I arrived in Congress, I waited for horses to disembark. Then I secured their leads and rode home. Papa worked with the herd, so I waited until supper to tell my parents how the trip went.

"She loves me," I started. I told them about the conversation with Uncle Adam.

"I think his request makes sense," Papa said. "I agree. We should all pray for your relationship."

Mama agreed as well.

———

THE WEEKS FLEW by. Penny wrote to me every few days. I wrote to her several times. The letters helped heal the hurt we both felt. It also gave us a chance to dream about our future. She confided she would much rather be a rancher's wife. I told her how much she meant to me.

Papa and the cowboys helped us build a home for my parents. They decided the existing ranch house felt too big for them. Mama said it was meant to hold a young family with lots of children, not an old married couple.

Though I was excited to see Penny again, the prospect of facing Greyson twisted my stomach. The more I prayed, the more convinced I became I needed to ask for his forgiveness. I doubted the two of us would be friends, since I had dealt with him unfairly. I treated Uncle Adam poorly, too.

The day before our trip, I sat down and wrote a letter to Greyson. I hoped he would not see it as the coward's way out. Hopefully, he would receive it well. Penny thought the letter was a good choice, so I took her advice.

Even though I apologized for ruining his future dreams, I held back from telling him I would do nothing different. I did what I had to do. Still, I needed to clear the air with him, so I apologized for disrespecting him.

When the afternoon of July third rolled around, I grinned ear to ear. A few days later, I would marry Penny. I could hardly wait.

CHAPTER 13

PENNY

I STOOD ON the train platform waiting for it to bring my love back to me. When I heard the whistle, I jumped up from the bench next to my father and started pacing.

Papa smiled at me. Over the weeks we were apart, Papa warmed to the idea of Nathan and me marrying. He told me last night he would bless our union, and that he was proud of me for doing as he asked.

I was glad he asked us to pray. Without prayer, I would not have asked Greyson to forgive me. Nathan would not have written a letter to Greyson. Though things remained strained between him and me, he appreciated that we both tried to smooth things over with him.

When Dory confided that she might have feelings for Greyson, I became doubly glad I didn't marry him. The four of us would have been miserable had I gone through with it. I would pray for Dory going forward.

"Hey!" Nathan said, stirring me from my thoughts.

I launched myself into his open arms. He brushed a quick kiss across my lips.

"I missed you so much," he whispered before he ran his fingers down my arm to intertwine with mine.

"I missed you too."

We rode back to the ranch together. Mama offered Caty's old room to Nathan's parents. Nathan agreed to stay at the bunkhouse for the few days before we married and I moved down to Congress.

That evening, Nathan saddled our horses. Then we rode up to our spot on the high trail overlooking the ranch and lake. He spread out a blanket for us.

As I sat next to him, I looped my arm around his. I let out a long sigh.

"I will miss this place," I said. "And my family."

"I know. There's nothing so beautiful. Except maybe you."

I nudged his side. "I might be?"

He turned to face me. A soft smile spread across his lips. "Yeah, just maybe."

I laughed. "Well, you're almost as handsome as this place."

His smile faded. The desire in his eyes sent my heart racing.

"Penny," he started as he took my hands. "I have loved you for longer than I can remember. You are my best friend. And you are more beautiful than a sunset on Colter Ranch. I love you completely. Though I'm sorry it took me almost too long to tell you, I'm glad I did. Will you be my wife?"

"I think you already know the answer to that question."

"Just humor me."

"Yes, of course, Nathan Cahill. I will be your wife."

Then, as the sun set, my love had only eyes for me. The kiss he gave me promised so much. My dream would come true in a few more days.

———

On July fifth, in a small private ceremony at our spot,

with only our parents and my sisters as witnesses, I stood before Nathan. I promised to love and obey him. I promised my whole heart, mind, and body to him. He promised the same.

Then I said my farewells to my family on the train station platform as I traveled with my husband to our new home. A home I'd never seen.

"You nervous?" he whispered as he looped an arm over my shoulder.

"I just realized I never asked about our house. I hope you aren't taking me to some shoddy, run-down shack."

He laughed. "No. It's a four-bedroom home. Nice sized kitchen and parlor. There is plenty of room for us and a few children."

My cheeks warmed at the glint in his eye. "Do your parents like their new house?"

"We only just finished it before traveling. They moved out of the bedroom, but still have other things to move."

As I leaned against his side, I watched the trees speed by. When the train moved its way down the mountain, the landscape opened up to a large, grassy valley.

"It's beautiful. I thought you said it wasn't."

"It's not as beautiful as Colter Ranch."

"I disagree. It's wonderful," I said. "I can hardly wait to see our home."

"Me either." His voice turned husky, sending shivers down my back.

Once the train stopped in Congress, we quickly retrieved the Cahill wagon from the livery and loaded up my things. His parents drove the wagon while I rode Cupcake, my parent's wedding gift to me. Nathan mounted Commodore. It warmed my heart that he chose him as his horse. The two made quite a pair.

As we neared the ranch, my breath caught. In the distance,

the blue-gray mountains broke up the deep blue sky. Grass covered acres of land. The two-story white house glimmered in the late afternoon sun. A few horses mingled in the corral. Off in the distance, the large herd kicked up dust.

"It's perfect, Nathan. I love it."

"Head in and freshen up. Mama said she'll cook up some supper at her new house. If we feel like joining them, we're welcome."

He took Cupcake's reins from me.

I hurried up the stairs and opened the door. My jaw slackened as I explored the house. It was huge and wonderful and perfect. Nathan caught up to me in the master bedroom.

"Glad to see you here," he teased before crossing the room to sweep me into his arms.

Before I thought of a witty retort, he captured my lips with his. Love for my husband filled my soul. Our wedding night ended blissfully. We never made it for supper at his parents' place.

EPILOGUE

February 14, 1894

NATHAN

"MORNING WIFE," I greeted Penny like I had every morning for six months.

She groaned and rolled over. "I'm so tired."

I frowned. It wasn't like her to sleep in. "Come on, Penny. Time to start the day."

She grabbed the blankets and pulled them over her head. Then, a few seconds later, she tossed them aside and ran for the washroom. My heart lurched as I listened to the sound of her gagging.

"Can I get you some water?" I asked through the door. "Do you need help?"

"No." She moaned. "I'll be down shortly."

My throat constricted as I headed to the kitchen. I started a fire in the stove. Then I went outside to gather some eggs. I knew how to cook toast and eggs.

Mama left the coop with a full basket. "Where's Penny?"

"She's sick. I thought I'd help with morning chores."

Mama's eyes grew round. "Sick? Hmm. Let me make breakfast. Can you let your father know to come over to your house?"

"Alright."

As we walked back to my house together, I couldn't shake off my anxiety. It bothered me Penny felt ill.

Yet, when I entered the kitchen, she sat at the table, fully dressed, sipping some tea. Her skin glowed as she offered me a sweet smile.

"Oh good. Everyone is here," she said. "Nathan, we have some exciting news to share."

"We do?"

She nodded. "Yes."

I frowned as I took a seat next to her.

"We're going to have a child."

My breath left in a rush. "A baby?"

She squealed. "Yes!"

"Congratulations, son," Papa said as he slapped me on the shoulder.

"When will the baby arrive?" Mama asked.

"Around June or July."

"A baby?" I asked again, as the news tried to penetrate my foggy mind.

Then I smiled. "A baby."

I pulled my wife into my arms and kissed her soundly as Mama set breakfast on the table. When Penny pulled back, I grinned. "A baby."

Penny laughed. "Yes, husband. A baby."

As soon as breakfast finished, my parents left. I lingered, not wanting to leave my wife just yet.

"I love you," I said as I helped her dry dishes.

"I love you, Nathan." She snorted. "It's hard to believe this time last year. I thought I lost you."

As I stored the last dried dish, I gazed into her eyes. "And I thought I'd lost you. Yet, I pursued you before it was too late. Look at us now."

She leaned against me and wrapped her arms behind my neck. "Happily married. Starting a family."

Then I lowered my lips to hers, expressing my tender love for my wife. I sent up a prayer of gratitude she was mine and I was hers forever.

IN LOVE
WITH THE
HORSE TRAINER

The path of the righteous is level;
you make level the way of the righteous.
In the path of your judgments,
O Lord, we wait for you;
your name and remembrance
are the desire of our soul.
My soul yearns for you in the night;
my spirit within me earnestly seeks you.
For when your judgments are in the earth,
the inhabitants of the world learn right-
eousness.

—Isaiah 26:7-9

CHAPTER I

Larson Stables
Near Prescott, Arizona Territory
February 14, 1894

DORY

MIDNIGHT. AS I shrugged my coat over my nightgown, sorrow overwhelmed my soul. I stuffed my feet in my boots. Then I grabbed an extra blanket and the lantern before I opened the door.

The sharp night air bit through my long coat, stinging my legs. Perhaps I should have taken the time to change. I had plenty of it since I was alone tonight.

My sweet older sisters had found the loves of their lives. Caty with her woodworking husband, Josiah. Three children now boasted their love. Penny finally reconnected with her love, Nathan. They married and moved away seven months ago, leaving a broken-hearted Greyson and a hopeful me behind.

Seven months had done little to change my feelings for Greyson. I fell more in love with him every day. And every day it appeared he might never notice me.

As I squared my shoulders, I set the blanket on a chair on the porch. Then I lit the lantern. For a few seconds, I considered sitting in the rocker instead of walking to the dock.

Unfortunately, the porch roof obscured my vision of the stars. I sighed, picked up the blanket, and trudged forward as a thin layer of snow crunched beneath my boots. When I glanced up at the sky, not a cloud marred the spectacular view of God's majestic starry night. I took a deep breath and stepped on to the dock.

As I let the air release from my lungs ever so slowly, I saw the fog it created in the dim light of the lantern. I strode to the end of the pier. Then I set the lantern down and shook out the blanket, settling it on the frigid wood planks. I eased myself down on the warm wool covering, leaned back, and wrapped it over my chilled legs.

Lord, I know you want me to remember you and desire you above all else. Tonight, I release to you the deepest desire of my heart: Greyson. He's everything I want in a husband. Yet, he does not notice me.

"I confess," I whispered into the frosty night air. The stars sparkled overhead like many nights before, nights where my sisters bared their souls to me and I to them. "I confess, Lord, that I've allowed my mind and heart to focus too much on Greyson. He is just like Papa, the dream You implanted in my heart as a young girl."

"But I think about him too much. Lord, I want Your name and remembrance to be the focus of my soul. I want to trust in You. I know You have a man in mind for me. Perhaps it is Greyson. Perhaps it is not."

My heart snagged on the admission. I knew I must let Greyson go. I must submit my heart to God first and trust in Him alone. A tear slid down my cheek and I wiped it away.

"I release Greyson Hastings to You. My love for you, God, should take the first place in my heart again. Let me serve You. Let the labor of my hands please You."

I closed my eyes and took a deep breath. As I exhaled the icy air from my lungs, I released my dreams and desires to the God and Creator of my heart and of these beautiful, starry nights. Then I opened my eyes.

"Dory? What are you doing out here?"

As I yelped, I jumped to my feet and took a step backward. Losing my balance, I tumbled over the edge of the dock into the freezing water below.

CHAPTER 2

GREYSON

THE BUNKHOUSE FELT too confining. I leaned over the edge of my bunk and grabbed a pair of trousers. Then I donned a shirt before I stuffed my arms in my coat. I quietly jammed my feet in my boots before I pushed off the bed.

Slowly, I opened the door and slipped out into the chilly night air. I walked toward the barn as my troubles rolled around in my mind.

At twenty-four, I was expecting to be married and have a child. An image of Penny came to mind. Then I shook my head. She married Nathan Cahill seven months ago. I must stop pining over what could never be. They were happy. They were truly in love.

I sighed as I ran a hand through my hair. I wasted too much time licking the wounds of my jilted heart. Not that I believed I had loved Penny all that deeply. She was beautiful and full of life. We had a good time together. But I didn't think we shared any soul-stirring romantic feelings. We were a good match. Yet nothing like the love Adam shared for Julia existed in my relationship with their daughter.

When I first sought the Larsons, my motives were to learn

from the best horse breeders and trainers in the territory. Their reputation spread far and wide, even up to my family's ranch near Flagstaff. I had no intention of finding a wife.

I had a gift, Mama said, with horses. I knew I didn't know as much as she thought. So, I sought the masters of their craft.

When Adam Larson responded to my letter inviting me to spend a year learning from him, I knew very little about him or his family. Once I arrived at Larson Stables, which was nestled in Colter Ranch, I discovered he and his wife shared a relationship I envied. They were a perfect match in their business. I had a hard time distinguishing what I learned from Adam versus what I learned from Julia, as they worked seamlessly together. When their middle daughter, Penny, showed an interest in working with horses at my side, I decided she might make a good helpmate for me.

I could not have been more wrong. Little did I know when I proposed to her that her heart had always belonged to Nathan Cahill. I meant nothing more to her than a mere distraction from her perceived rift with him. Though she believed she loved me for a time, I knew better as I reflected on our time together. I don't think I loved her so much as the idea of her being like her mother, Julia. She liked me well enough. But love? Not really.

As I gazed over the lake, a dim yellow light hooked my attention. Someone lay on the dock. My heart sank when I saw the still form, thinking the person was in distress. As I neared the pier, I realized Dory lay at the edge. Her soft voice carried on the still night air, causing my feet to slow.

"I confess, Lord," she said into the darkness, "that I've allowed my mind and heart to focus too much on Greyson."

My feet planted firmly at the sound of my name on her tongue. The words wrapped themselves around my soul and squeezed tight as understanding took shape. Dory fancied me.

Me. A man who completely ignored her for nearly a year.

I sighed. I wasn't discourteous or anything. The young woman worked harder than any woman I'd ever met. She managed all the meals for her parents, me, and Penny when she lived there. Dory cleaned all the laundry, kept the house, baked special desserts, and still found time for the occasional horse ride or errand at the stables. All of it was done with a gracious heart and an endearing smile.

"He is just like Papa, the dream You implanted in my heart as a young girl."

I swallowed hard against the lump in my throat. She thought I was like her Papa, a man I aspired to be like, but felt I so often fell short of emulating. And what did she mean by a dream God implanted in her heart as a young girl?

A conversation with Penny came to mind. I remembered she told me she and her sisters had a tradition. They went to the dock once a year. They shared their dreams and prayed over them under a blanket of stars. Hadn't she said it was on Valentine's Day?

Oh, wait! Since the hour rolled past midnight before I slipped from the bunkhouse, that meant today was the day.

Dory's sniffles broke my heart.

"I release Greyson Hastings to You."

My heart plummeted at the utter despair in her voice. I felt nothing other than friendly affection for her. Yet, those words stirred something deep within me. Something that begged me to keep her from releasing me forever.

I steeled myself against the foolish ideas running around in my head. Then I approached her.

When I looked down at her, the lantern cast a soft yellow glow across her beautiful face. Such smooth skin. Her long blond hair shone in the low light as it sprawled around her head. Though her eyes were closed, I knew their color, a lovely green that glistened when she smiled at me.

As she exhaled a deep breath, those amazing green eyes revealed themselves to me. My heart nearly stopped. I cleared my throat.

"Dory? What are you doing out here? It's freezing."

A frightened squeal escaped those darling lips as she shot to her feet. She took a step back, and I watched in dismay as her left foot missed the pier altogether. Before I reached for her, the sound of a splash rose to greet me.

I dropped to my knees and leaned over the edge of the dock.

"Dory!"

My stomach tightened as I weighed my options. I could dive in after her. Yet, I knew her to be a strong swimmer. She might need my help to lift her up to the dock. It would be hard if we were both shivering and soaked.

"Dory? Are you alright?"

"G-g-g-rey-son?"

I let out the breath I had been holding as her teeth chattered.

"Here." I thrust my hand out.

"I'm n-n-not decent."

I frowned. She needed to get out of that bone-chilling water. Who cared if she was decent?

"B-b-lan-k-ket?"

"Yes, it's here. Can you use the ladder? I'll hold up the blanket. I promise I won't look."

"Th-ank-k you."

As soon as I felt her push against the blanket, I wrapped my arms around her. Her body convulsed. I had to get her inside immediately. So, I did the only thing that came to mind. I swept her into my arms and ran toward her house with no consideration for anything besides getting her to safety.

Warmth flooded my soul at the feel of her in my arms.

Confusion threatened to cloud my mind. I forced myself to stuff down the feelings, stirring with brilliant clarity. I had to get her to the fireplace to prevent her from getting sick before the chill set in. I'd deal with the emotions later.

CHAPTER 3

DORY

WHEN I LANDED in the lake, the icy water sucked all the air from my lungs. As my coat soaked up lake water, it grew heavy, pulling me under. I kicked my feet hard, accidentally loosening my untied boots from my feet.

Air. I needed air.

I tore off my coat and let it sink. Then I pushed my arms down and kicked my legs with all my might until my head broke through the surface. Life-giving air filled my lungs in a gulp.

Within seconds, my teeth chattered against the frosty cold. I swam to the dock ladder. Before I started climbing the ladder, I stopped with one hand resting on a rung.

Greyson stood on the pier. Before I fell in, I saw something thrilling and confusing written on his face. Then I startled and splashed backward into the water. I could not hardly climb out in front of him clad in a soaked clingy nightgown. It would not be proper.

I stuttered his name through my shivers. Then I confirmed my blanket lay dry on the dock. After he promised not to look, I climbed out of the lake. The night air pricked my drenched skin. Try as I might, I could not stop trembling. My teeth clicked loudly as they vibrated against each other uncontrollably. It seemed to take hours before the warmth of the blanket enveloped me.

Before I blinked, Greyson lifted me into his muscular arms. I soaked in his heat while his nearness sent my senses racing. My heart pounded a quick beat against my chest. As I gulped for air, the scent of horses, hay, and something distinctly Greyson filled my lungs. I'd never been so close to him before and I quite liked it, despite my tremors.

He quickly opened the door to my home. Then he laid me on the floor by the waning fire. I could barely think as the cold seeped deep into my bones.

Once he shrugged out of his coat, he laid it over me. Then he snatched a throw from a nearby sofa and spread across me. He grabbed a few logs and added them to the fire, determined to bring it to life again.

"Greyson?" Papa's voice sounded confused. Then he growled out the next words. "What are you doing in my house? What happened to my daughter?"

"Dory?" Mama's concern drew me away from Papa's scowling face.

Greyson failed to answer as he poked at the fire, trying to get the newest logs to catch. Papa clamped a hand down on his shoulder and jerked him around.

"Dory fell in the lake," he said matter-of-factly.

"Are you alright?" Mama said as she placed a hand on my cheek. "You're frozen!"

Mama's murmurings drowned out a heated discussion between Papa and Greyson.

"Adam!" Mama snapped him out of the argument. "Get her a change of clothes. We must get her out of these wet things. But I don't want to move her away from the fire."

Greyson said something about taking his leave, but Papa

had other ideas.

"I'm not done with you yet. Take a seat at the table. We'll finish this when I know Dory is on the mend."

"Let me start some tea," Mama said. "I'll be right back."

I closed my eyes as my body shivered.

When Papa returned with another nightgown and robe, he helped me to my feet. Then he held the blanket to block any view of me while Mama peeled the chilly wet garment from me. Then she helped me into fresh clothes before she wrapped a dry blanket around me.

"You can lower it," she said as she led me to the chair closest to the fire. She took each of my feet and placed thick wool stockings over them.

Papa handed me a mug of hot tea before he turned toward Greyson. From my vantage point near the fire, I watched the exchange between the two men who meant the world to me.

"What were you doing with my daughter near the lake?"

Greyson's dark brown eyes locked with Papa's as his brow creased. He ran a hand through his jet-black hair.

"It's not what you think."

"Explain it then."

"I couldn't sleep, so I dressed and headed toward the barn when I noticed a lantern on the dock. As I went to investigate, I found Dory, um, praying."

Heat flamed my face to the point my cheeks stung. Certainly, no cold skin remained there. How much had he overheard?

"I didn't realize that was what she was doing until I walked closer. At first, I thought she might be injured. When I figured out she was fine, my curiosity got the better of me. I ended up startling her."

He turned those handsome chocolate brown eyes my way. "I'm so sorry. I didn't mean to… invade your privacy or frighten you."

I gave him a tentative smile as my shivering subsided.

"She jumped up and before I could steady her, she inadvertently tumbled over the edge of the pier and landed in the lake." Then Greyson's gaze shifted to me before he asked, "What happened to your coat?"

"It grew too heavy. Both my coat and boots are at the bottom of the lake."

Papa's scowl remained fixed in place. "Are you telling me you saw... Saw my daughter..."

"No, Papa. Greyson saw nothing. He held up a blanket for me and acted the gentleman, rushing me in here as quickly as possible."

I glanced at Greyson and smiled. "Thank you."

He gave a sharp nod. When his eyes held my gaze, they softened. I wondered again how much of my prayer he overheard. I couldn't remember what I had whispered aloud.

After I tore my eyes away from Greyson, I caught Papa studying me intently. My throat constricted at the fire burning in his stare. I was an obedient daughter. Made my parents proud. So, when his expression turned to disappointment, I bowed my head, the pain of it too raw. Tears silently leaked from my eyes.

"Sir, Dory did nothing wrong," Greyson came to my defense.

"Leave." Papa's voice held a steely edge, which left no room for an argument. "We'll speak in the morning."

Greyson shot to his feet and darted from our home, leaving his coat behind.

Once I finished a second cup of tea, Mama helped me to bed. She left the door cracked open after she turned down the lamp.

As my parents' voices floated on the air, I stared at the ceiling and strained to listen.

"I have half a mind to make him marry her," Papa said.

"Adam, don't be rash. Seven months ago, he was about to marry Penny. Do you really think he's been harboring a secret passion for Dory?"

Silence stretched for a few minutes.

"Regardless of the past several months, the way he looked at her tonight… I was a young man once. I know what that look means."

Mama sighed loudly. "Have you forgotten how you and I traveled to Arizona?"

I leaned closer to the edge of my bed, not being familiar with how my parents moved here.

"That's not the same thing."

"We shared a tent on a wagon train and posed as brother and sister for weeks."

My eyes widened.

"You and I know nothing untoward happened between us," Mama said.

"I know exactly how hard it was not to pull you into my arms every night. I loved you even then."

"But you didn't. And when my brother accused you of impropriety, you proved your character."

Papa grunted.

"You know Greyson is an honorable man. I have no reason to doubt what he says is true. Dory contradicted nothing he said."

"What was she thinking when she went to the dock alone?" Papa asked.

Mama sighed. "The girls have done that for a while."

"What?!" Papa lowered his voice. "What do you mean? Why didn't you say anything?"

"It was harmless. They gazed at the stars, dreamed about their futures, and prayed over it together. Was it odd they sneaked out late at night to do so? Certainly. But it was completely innocent."

"How long have known about this?"

"I think Dory was twelve the first time I caught them."

Mama knew we did that? How much had she heard over the years? Heat warmed my face as I thought about it.

"I only watched from the porch when I caught them. Never listened. And I ducked back in before they started walking back. I made sure they returned to their beds and never breathed a word."

Their voices grew silent for a few minutes.

"Adam, it's sweet that the girls kept the tradition. They remained close because they shared their secrets. I'm not sorry I let them continue it."

Papa sighed. "What do I do now?"

I didn't hear Mama's response because their bedroom door clicked shut.

As I closed my eyes, I let out a long breath. I did not look forward to morning. So much had changed tonight. I wasn't certain how I'd ever look Greyson in the face again. My parents, or at least Papa, were disappointed with me. I wished I could run far away.

CHAPTER 4

GREYSON

As I TRUDGED back to the bunkhouse in the dark night, I stuffed my hands in my pockets. Despite the bite in the air and having left my coat at the Larson's, I stopped by the pier. I picked up the flickering lantern before turning toward the bunkhouse.

Dory harbored secret feelings for me.

A smile twitched in the corner of my mouth. Dory had been right in front of me. Perhaps I had completely missed the signs and picked the wrong sister.

Before I opened the door to the bunkhouse, I extinguished the lantern. When I stepped inside, I kicked off my boots and flopped down on my bunk.

The look in her eyes when she thanked me. My heart warmed just thinking about it. Then I stifled a chuckle. Even with her damp, ratty hair, she still projected a sweet charm. I had noticed before but had been so absorbed in my pain over losing Penny that I ignored it.

When I yawned, I rolled onto my side, trying to quiet my churning thoughts so I could get some sleep.

The next morning, I woke to the noise of the bunkhouse, having slept only a few hours. After I readied for the day, I headed toward the Larson's home with the lantern in hand. The cool morning air sliced through my shirt, and I wished I had grabbed my coat before I left last night.

With my hand on the doorknob, I paused. After the events of the night before, the family may not welcome me. Adam's short fuse surprised me. I hoped he'd calmed down.

"Morning!"

I jumped at the sound of Dory's voice behind me. When I held the door open for her, I noticed she wore my coat. She wore wool stockings over her feet. No shoes. Guilt kicked my gut. She lost her boots and coat in the lake because I startled her. I needed to rectify that situation today.

"I hope you don't mind me borrowing your coat," she said as she slipped past me with a full basket of eggs. "I will have breakfast ready in a few minutes. Please come in."

I placed the basket on the table near the door. Then I helped her out of my coat.

"I'll go feed the horses then," I said as I shrugged into my coat.

"Perfect."

As I closed the door and headed to the barn, she smiled at me. The sweet scent of honey and cinnamon lingered on my coat. I breathed it in as I tried to sort through the emotions flooding back from the night before. Dory in my arms, shivering. Her sincere gratitude for my help, even though I caused her to fall into the lake.

After picking up a bucket, I scooped up oats. Then I went through the motions of feeding the horses.

Though I hadn't planned a trip to town, I knew I should pick up a new coat for Dory. And some boots. It was the least I could do to make up for last night's disaster. I wondered if she could borrow some shoes and a coat from Julia or her cousin Violet. Surely, she'd want to pick out the new items herself. A smile stretched across my lips. She might enjoy a break from her routine.

Once I finished caring for the horses, I walked back to the Larson home. When I opened the door, the smell of fried potatoes and bacon greeted me. My stomach growled as I took my usual seat at the table. Across from Dory.

She flashed me another bright smile as she set out the food. Then she grabbed my mug and filled it with coffee, black and steaming hot.

When I glanced at Adam, his eyes narrowed. I quickly bowed my head, waiting for him to say grace. Julia gave the blessing instead, which caused me concern. Adam always prayed over meals. Not his wife.

After a chorus of "amens," I cleared my throat.

"I thought I ought to take Dory to town to replace her coat and boots. I mean… It was my fault…"

"How thoughtful," Julia said. She turned her attention to Dory. "You can borrow my coat and boots. I must catch up on some paperwork."

"Thank you, Mama."

Adam grunted but didn't voice an objection.

As soon as breakfast finished, I stood and offered to saddle Dory's horse.

"I'll walk with you," Adam said.

My throat constricted as we walked to the barn.

"Dory confirmed your version of events."

Of course she did. It was the truth.

"I'm not pleased about what happened."

"Nothing untoward happened."

"So she said."

As I brushed down Shadow, Adam groomed Dory's horse, Cookie. After several glares, I paused.

"Do you want to say something?" I asked as I smoothed a

blanket over Shadow's back.

Adam cleared his throat. "I thought I might, but not really. Thank you for taking her to town."

"It's the least I can do."

"You can put her things on my account."

I shook my head. "I insist on replacing her lost items. I feel terrible about startling her."

Adam sighed. "Fine."

While I saddled Shadow, the tension in the room faded. I hoped Adam would forgive me for whatever perceived wrongs he assumed I committed. I was doing the best I could to right the wrong.

I led the horses to the house. When Dory opened the door, I helped her onto Cookie's back. That same honey cinnamon fragrance wafted from her. I liked it.

After I climbed into my saddle, we rode up the lane to-ward town.

"I'm very sorry, Dory. I still can't believe that happened."

When I glanced at her, her cheeks turned pink.

"Thank you for riding with me to town."

"I mean to do more than that. I'll replace what you lost."

"Thank you."

"Was your father upset with you?"

Dory let out a loud breath. "Considerably. Until Mama re-minded him of, as she phrased it, their 'journey west'. I don't know what that means, but Papa frowned and pursed his lips when she said it."

I cleared my throat as I considered telling her what I over-heard the night before. That she thought I was a good man like her father and that she released me. No. It would only make things awkward between us. Perhaps it'd be better if I focused on getting to know her better. The glimpse of her heart and prayers last night intrigued me.

"I really enjoyed the apple tarts you made for dessert last night," I said.

"Oh. Thank you."

She looked down at her hands as her cheeks reddened. A twinge of guilt poked at my heart. I took her for granted. Perhaps all of us had.

"I enjoy baking."

I chuckled. "And I love eating the wonderful things you bake."

"What else do you like?" I asked.

Her eyes widened as they traveled to mine. My breath lodged in my throat. How could I have overlooked her?

CHAPTER 5

DORY

GREYSON'S QUESTION LEFT me stunned. First compliments. Then a sincere interest in what I liked. If I didn't know better, I might hope he wanted to learn more about me. I resisted the urge to shake my head. It was only polite conversation. I should not read into it.

I sucked in a breath before I answered. "When spring comes, I enjoy long walks hunting for wildflowers and absorbing the beauty of the ranch."

"What else?"

My belly fluttered. The sun warmed my back, and his brown eyes warmed my cheeks for the dozenth time since we started toward town. I bit my lip. Maybe, just maybe... I wouldn't let the thought fully form. Afraid to believe it.

"In the evening, I often read. Seems I can never find enough books to read. Someday maybe we'll have a library. Could you imagine? Books galore to borrow any time I wanted?"

"Perhaps you could start a book exchange?" he suggested.

"A book exchange. You mean something more than me and Violet swapping books?" Slowly I nodded. "Women in the area might like to exchange books."

I grinned as the excitement built.

"That's a great idea, Greyson. I know who to talk to on Sunday."

"Any time."

Any time? My pulse raced. Did he mean it?

When we arrived in town, I reined in my horse near The O.K. Store. I snickered every time I stopped at the store. Their goods were better than okay, and I found it funny the owner chose that name.

"Let me help you," Greyson said as he rushed to my side.

Then he lifted his hands to my waist, something he'd never done before. As his fingers curled around me, my breath caught. I rested my hands on his shoulders. The scent of his shaving soap heightened my senses. Tingles shot through my arms as he lowered me down. When my feet rested on the ground, his hands lingered. So did mine. Those dark brown eyes roamed over my face like a soft caress. My lips felt dry, and I licked them.

He cleared his throat and offered me his arm, so I rested my hand in the crook, still unnerved by his nearness. Whatever that was, I hoped he felt it, too.

As he held the door for me, he said that he would be back in a few minutes. "Take your time."

"Alright."

"And, Dory, don't put this on your father's account. I'll take care of it when I return."

A tentative smile drew up one side of my face. I told the clerk what I needed after walking down the aisle. After trying on two different pairs of boots, I picked one and left them on. The clerk agreed to hold Mama's boots and coat at the front for me.

Then I found the coats. A lovely emerald-green one called to me. The full-length wool covering would keep me warm. And it brought out the green in my eyes. I heard Mama's voice scolding me in my head to choose something more practical. Practical to Mama translated to boring to me. The emerald coat would keep me warm and looked stylish. A brown or black coat only met the first requirement.

I sighed as I shrugged out of the emerald one and reached for a brown.

"Did you not like it?" Greyson asked, startling me.

"It's not practical."

He frowned. "What's not practical about it? It fits you to perfection. You looked lovely in it. And it would keep you as warm as any of these others."

My hand hovered mid-air, almost touching the brown one.

"Come on, try it on again."

Greyson reached for the green coat and held it for me. I slid my arms into the sleeves. When he dropped it onto my shoulders, his hands rested lightly there. The heat of his nearness sent pulses down my back as he looked over my shoulder into the mirror.

"I think you should get this one, if you like it."

I liked the way I looked. The reflection of us standing together felt like home. We looked good together. And the new glimmer in his eyes warmed me.

"Are you sure? I can find one cheaper."

A frown flitted across his features before a smile replaced it. He turned to the clerk, who stood nearby. "We'll take it."

While I looked at my reflection, he paid for the purchase. It was a lovely coat. A smile stretched across my lips. Something good came out of me falling into the lake.

"Ready?" Greyson asked, coming up next to me.

As I nodded, I held my breath. His hand slid down to clasp mine. He held Mama's shoes and her coat rested over his arm.

"I know it's early for lunch. Do you want some coffee before we leave?"

"I… I'd like that."

We stopped by my horse, and he stowed my mother's things. Then he grasped my hand again as he led me to the café. Once the server led us to a table, Greyson held out a chair for me. Then he sat across from me.

"Two coffees, please. Would you like some cinnamon rolls or anything else?"

"That sounds delightful."

My heart raced under his intense stare while he ordered the cinnamon rolls. Then I frowned. Perhaps he overheard my declaration last night, and that was why he acted so strangely.

"Why are you behaving oddly today?" I braved the question.

CHAPTER 6

GREYSON

"AM I?" I TRIED to deflect Dory's question, knowing full well my behavior must seem strange to her. Something shifted in my heart after her secret declaration last night. My perspective changed. I became more aware of her and her heart.

In the store, as she hesitated over the less expensive coat, I ran through what she must have been thinking. That she wasn't worth the prettier coat, the one that brought a smile to her face and a light to her eyes. Her expressions morphed as she set it back on the rack and reached for the brown one. She was wrong. She was worth the pretty green coat and so much more. I had been so blind, wrapped up in myself.

She narrowed those lovely green eyes. "Last night, what did you hear?"

My eyes darted away. "Enough." Enough to make me see her.

"I see. So you know that I… That I…"

"Fancy me? Yes."

A frown creased her forehead as she reached for her coat and stood. I grabbed her hand.

"Please sit. Let's enjoy our coffee and treat."

Dory slowly eased back down onto her chair.

Once the coffee and cinnamon rolls arrived, I swallowed my pride.

"I confess," I said. "I took you for granted because I was so caught up in what happened with Penny."

Her green eyes sparked as she lifted her coffee to her lips.

"I've wallowed for far too long. I was outside last night for that reason. On my way to the barn to contemplate my life, I spotted you on the pier. My curiosity got the better of me."

As rosy circles graced her cheeks, she picked at the cinnamon rolls.

I let out a loud breath. "If you are interested, I'd like to court you, Dory."

Her eyes widened. "Me? Whatever for?"

"You are beautiful. Kind. A wonderful homemaker. A godly woman."

She snorted, then shook her head. She muttered, "You heard what I said."

Then she straightened her back and continued. "While I appreciate your praise, Greyson, I'm not looking for a job. I want the man who courts me to love me. You do not."

Her green eyes speared me.

"But I could. The point of courting is to determine if we might be a good match. If we get along well and develop feelings for one another."

Dory pursed her lips as a shadow fell over her features.

"You're still in love with Penny."

I shook my head. "Honestly, I don't know if I ever was. Not really."

The silence lingered between us, so I popped a large bite of cinnamon roll into my mouth. It was good, but not as good as Dory's.

"Is this about Larson Stables?"

I frowned. "No. This is about you and me. I didn't come to

Prescott hoping to take over your parents' business. I came to learn from them. My intention from the beginning has always been to return to Flagstaff and start my breeding and training business. I never considered taking over Larson Stables until your father mentioned it to me after... Well, it doesn't matter. That's all in the past now."

She ripped off a corner of a cinnamon roll and chewed it slowly. After studying me for what seemed like hours, she dropped her gaze back to the cinnamon roll.

I don't know what I had hoped would happen with our conversation. The idea of courting her just came out. Perhaps I bungled it, making her feel like my back-up plan, judging by her questions. That had not been my intent.

The silence grew uncomfortable.

"Tell me what you're thinking," I said as I reached for her hand. When she didn't pull hers away, I was content to keep holding it.

"I... I don't want to be your second choice." She looked out the window. "My heart won't withstand that kind of pain."

"Dory." I rubbed my thumb across her knuckles. "You aren't my second choice."

"Before last night, you barely noticed me, so how can I believe anything else?"

"Will you give me a chance? Spend more time with me if we do not court officially. Get to know me."

She was right. I had not given her the time of day before. Still, I wanted a chance.

"We should head back. I didn't expect to be gone so long. I need to return home to start lunch."

As I withdrew my hand from hers, I hoped she might change her mind. I paid for the coffee and cinnamon rolls. Then I offered my arm to Dory. Her light touch seared through my coat. Things would never return to the way they were before I heard her prayers. I would win her heart. No matter what it took.

CHAPTER 7

DORY

GREYSON MEANT HIS words to be a compliment. I knew it. Still, my heart rejected them. Kind. Beautiful. Godly. A good homemaker. Nothing about love or affection. So, of course, I felt second best. Worse yet, second best to my sister Penny, his former fiancée.

Though, if I was honest with myself, I often felt that way compared to my sisters. Caty had all the traits of a perfect wife and mother. Compassionate. Infinitely patient.

Then there was Penny. She was outgoing and competitive. She could do anything with horses. A perfect match for Nathan. No matter what I did, I could never live up to her. Not in Greyson's eyes. He loved her spunky nature. He liked that she had worked the horses with him. I knew it to be true because both spoke of it during their brief engagement.

So, to hear Greyson list homemaker as one of my fine attributes chafed. While it was true, it failed to compare to Penny's love and talent with horses. I wouldn't help Greyson that way. I wanted to be loved and cherished for who I was and not what I could do. Greyson didn't know me well enough to love me.

Sure, a courtship meant learning more about each other. To court with no love or affection? A tear slipped down my cheek. Why did he hear my prayer? Why had I spoken the words aloud?

I kicked Cookie to the top of the lane as the ranch came into view. I really ought to get something prepared for lunch.

When I dismounted my horse, I led it into the stable. As I unbuckled the cinch, Greyson told me he'd see to my horse. So, I grabbed Mama's boots and coat from the saddlebags and hurried across the yard.

The smell of freshly baked bread greeted me as I opened the door. Papa sat at the table next to Mama, both with a plate of half-eaten sandwiches in front of them.

"Dory, welcome back," Papa said.

Mama smiled. "That's a lovely coat. It really brings out the color of your eyes."

"Thank you," I replied as I hung her coat on its usual hook. Then I dropped her boots on the floor nearby.

"Are you hungry? I made extras for you and Greyson."

I poured myself a cup of coffee and joined them at the table. "Greyson is caring for the horses."

"It looks like the trip was a success," Papa said.

I nodded as I reached for a sandwich. "I'll get started cleaning as soon as lunch is over."

"No need to hurry with it, if you'd like to relax this afternoon. I know you were up late."

"Your mother is right. Why don't you take a break this afternoon?"

I sighed. "Alright. I'll plan supper and then maybe I'll walk around the lake or go see what Violet is doing."

Mama patted my hand. Even though she meant it to be a soothing action, it bothered me right then. I wasn't a little girl. I was a woman with responsibilities. It should have been me fixing the midday meal. Not Mama.

Mama sighed. "Someday you'll have a home of your own. I appreciate what you do for us. But I'm afraid I've relied on you more than I should."

"I don't mind. What else would I do with my time?"

"Still, I don't want you to deny yourself an opportunity because you're worried about taking care of us. I helped with the horses before you or your sisters were old enough to help with chores. Occasionally, I relied on help from Betty or Hannah."

As soon as I finished eating, I grabbed my Bible and a blanket. Then I headed out as Greyson entered.

"Excuse me," I mumbled as I pushed past him, annoyed by how much his presence unsettled me.

I hurried to the pier. After I laid out the blanket, I sat down. Closing my eyes, I breathed deeply. As I let it out slowly, I opened my eyes. Had it really been last night that I gazed up at the stars and released Greyson? I promised to let the Lord be the deepest desire of my heart. I would remember Him, not the man who failed to notice me.

In less than a day, that man suddenly noticed me and asked to court me. Did God cause Greyson to fall in love with me so soon? I shook my head. Greyson didn't love me. He only just realized I existed.

When I opened my Bible, I turned to Isaiah 26 and reread the verses from yesterday that prompted me to recommit my soul-deep pondering to focus on God.

"The path of the righteous is level; you make level the way of the righteous. In the path of your judgments, O Lord, we wait for you; your name and remembrance are the desire of our soul. My soul yearns for you in the night; my spirit within me earnestly seeks you. For when your judgments are in the earth, the inhabitants of the world learn righteousness."

Lord, I do want to follow Your Will for my life. What should I do?

My eyes dropped to the page. *In the path of your judgments, O Lord, we wait for you…*

Wait for the Lord. That must be the answer. Just like I prayed last night, I ought to let the Lord's name and remembrance be the desire of my soul. Stop thinking about Greyson. Wait for the Lord.

Taking no action seemed hard. Waiting for the Lord meant not worrying about my circumstances. Not trying to take control of things. Waiting meant trusting the God of all Creation. The same God who spoke the world into existence. The same God who hung the stars in the sky had the power to work in my life and my heart. All I should focus on was responding to what He set before me.

And waiting on Him was it.

CHAPTER 8

May 14, 1894

DORY

THREE MONTHS PASSED since I fell in the lake and turned over the desires of my heart to God. Nothing changed with my circumstances. My heart still longed for love. But my soul rested in the peace of waiting, though some days required me to turn to God again for the strength to wait.

Greyson hadn't asked to court me again. We settled into a polite friendship. He thanked me more often and complimented my cooking. Sometimes, he mentioned how lovely I looked. But nothing more passed between us.

Wait for the Lord.

I sighed. I would wait.

My twenty-first birthday was in four days. Ironically, Greyson's twenty-fifth birthday was the same day, a fact I learned the previous year. I flipped through my cookbook, looking for the perfect cake recipe. If nothing else, I'd bake him a cake.

"Dory."

Greyson's deep voice broke me from my thoughts. I glanced at the clock. Half-past two. He came to the house at an unusual time. I turned to face him. My eyes scanned for signs of injury.

Seeing none, I allowed my gaze to linger on his. He shifted from foot to foot, gripping his hat in his hand.

"I was wondering if you would allow me to take you to dinner in town on Friday for your birthday. You work hard and never take time for yourself. I'd… I really want to treat you to something special."

My pulse throbbed as I blinked, not once, but twice.

He stepped closer and set his hat on the table. Then he took my hands in his.

"You are an amazing woman. Let me do this one thing for you."

Still no claim of affection. I pushed the thought aside.

"Alright. What time should I be ready?"

Greyson grinned. "Four o'clock? We can take the carriage, so you'll be comfortable."

Then he leaned forward and kissed my cheek. "I'll see you then."

I laughed softly. "You will still dine with us tonight?"

He chuckled. "Of course. Sorry."

As he backed toward the door, something seemed different in his gaze, his reluctance to break eye contact. Then he turned and left the house.

I fanned my face with a hand, suddenly feeling warm. Then I turned my attention back to the recipes. I'd still bake a cake for him. We would either eat it at lunch or after our dinner out.

———

"YOU LOOK GORGEOUS," cousin Violet said as she finished fixing my hair for me.

I looked at my reflection in the mirror and agreed. The pale green dress brought out the green in my eyes. The neckline showed off my delicate shoulders tastefully. Violet left a few ringlets of my golden blond hair at the sides, tickling my exposed shoulders and framing my face. The rest of my normally straight, long blond locks trailed down my back in soft curls. She had a gift for arranging hair.

"If he doesn't notice you tonight, then he's completely blind."

"He did ask me to go to dinner with him."

"I know. You're finally going on an actual date. Here," she said as she handed me a shawl. "In case you get chilled."

I rested the shawl over my arm for the time being. Then I stepped from my room ten minutes before four.

Mama looked up from the stove. She wiped her hands on a towel. Then she stood before me and took my hands in hers.

"You look so beautiful. Enjoy your time this evening. And don't worry about hurrying back. If need be, the cake will still be good tomorrow."

"Thanks, Mama."

"Your father will be here shortly. He wants to see you before you go."

I draped the shawl over the chair. Then I debated whether to sit down. I didn't want to wrinkle the silk dress.

"Dory," Papa greeted me. "My, look at what a lovely woman you've grown into."

His eyes misted a little before he placed a kiss on my cheek.

"Have a good time this evening."

"Thank you, Papa."

When a knock sounded on the door, Papa opened it. Greyson stepped over the threshold and my breath lodged in my throat. He wore a new suit and a fancy bowler hat instead of his cowboy hat. A soft smile stretched across his lips as he removed his hat and stepped closer. He shaved again, revealing his wonderfully angled jaw. Those dark eyes studied me for several minutes as heat crept up my face.

Then he held out his hand. I grabbed my shawl with one hand and took his hand with my other. He leaned down and placed a kiss on it. When he stood upright, he smiled.

"You look stunning, Dory."

I glanced down as my face warmed.

"Shall I help you with your shawl?"

He held out his hand, and I gave him the shawl. I didn't really need it, but I allowed him to rest it on my shoulders, anyway. When he gently gathered my hair, so it laid over the shawl, my heart raced frantically from the intimate gesture. Then he offered his arm and led me to the carriage before he rounded the carriage and sat next to me. Then he clucked the horse into motion.

"Is that a new dress? I don't recall you wearing it to church before."

I fidgeted with the edge of my shawl. "Yes."

"It's very nice."

When we reached the top of the lane out of the ranch, my pulse calmed some, though I savored Greyson's closeness. A date. I was actually going on a date with him. He finally asked me to go on an outing.

He asked about the book exchange.

"My cousin Lily helped organize it and she set aside a bookshelf in her house to hold the books. She has a notebook by it so women can sign out the books."

"Sounds like the beginning of a library. Have you read any good books lately?"

"Ellie Mae let me read her latest manuscript. It's amazing. I think it appeals to both men and women. The right mix of romance and action. She's so talented."

"I don't know how she writes with four children under foot."

"I'm sure that's why she holds to the early bedtime for them. Though Sterling just turned five in January and is fussing about it."

Greyson tucked my hand on his arm. "How many children do you want?"

My heart snagged on the question. "I... Ideally, three seems the perfect number. I suppose that's because my sisters and I have always been close and I wish the same for mine, if I'm graced with any."

"Three sounds like a nice number. Boys? Girls?"

I laughed. "I'll be happy with whatever God graces..."

I almost said 'us with.' That he brought up the conversation had me leaping too far ahead. I ought to tread lightly.

"I'd like at least one boy. Most men want their name to be carried on for generations."

"Really? Do you think Papa is disappointed in me?"

Greyson angled to look at me. "Why would you think that? He loves you so much. He's very proud of you."

"But I was his last hope for a son."

Greyson pulled the carriage to a stop. He set the brake and secured the reins. Then he turned to face me.

"Why do you do that?"

I licked my dry lips. "Do what?"

"Assume you are less than... That you aren't the most wonderful woman?"

My eyes darted away. "I'm nothing special. I'm a third daughter and have never shown an interest in the family business. My parents live and breathe Larson Stables."

Greyson lifted my chin. "You are special, Dory."

Then he leaned closer. My heart pounded in my ears as his lips brushed softly across mine. I closed my eyes as he repeated the sweet caress. When I sensed he leaned back, I finally opened my eyes.

"You are wonderful, just as you are," he whispered. "Beautiful beyond words, inside and out. You are a woman of character. You are so devoted to those you love."

Then he rested his forehead against mine.

"And I'm falling in love with you."

Me? Greyson falling in love with me?

His hand settled lightly on the back of my neck while his thumb softly stroked my jawline, sending thrilling shivers throughout my body. I thought he might kiss me again. Oh, how I wanted his kisses.

Instead, he straightened and gave me a saucy grin. "We ought to continue on to dinner."

"Uh, huh."

I rested my hand on his arm as he started the horse toward town again, excited to see what else might transpire through the evening.

CHAPTER 9

GREYSON

THOUGH IT TOOK me three months to ask Dory to supper, I had not wasted the time. I spend much time in prayer, trying to figure out how to move forward with her. Once I dealt with my wounded heart, I knew I was ready to see Dory for who she was.

And what a wonderful woman.

When her father opened the door and I saw her standing in that dress, I knew I'd be the worst kind of fool not to pursue her, to win her heart and give her mine. I realized I didn't truly want a woman to work horses with me. I wanted a woman who cared for me above all others, save God. The image of my future wife solidified in my mind, and it was her. A godly woman. A good homemaker. A sweet woman who cared for the needs of her family.

I had been foolish to ignore her. The more I learned about her, the more I saw how far superior she was compared to Penny. In fact, Dory reminded me of my mother. A woman who led her home with grace and kindness. Mama took care of our needs and managed her home with efficiency. I saw the same traits in Dory.

It hurt my heart when Dory said negative things about herself. I didn't understand why she always saw others as better than herself. I was aware of the verse. But it meant not to be arrogant. Dory didn't have an arrogant or assuming bone in her body. Instead, she saw herself as nothing special. That would be something I would help her see differently if she'd allow me.

After I pulled back from the tender moment in the carriage, I resolved anew to win her heart and to treasure her.

When we arrived at the restaurant, I escorted her to the secluded table I reserved. A part of me wished I could propose to her tonight. We had too much ground to cover before she would believe the sincerity of my heart. Hopefully, my plans for the birthday outing would be something she remembered for a long time.

After we ordered, I slid my first gift for her across the table.

"What's this?" she asked.

"Your birthday gift."

She took the package and pulled on the string. Then she removed the brown paper wrapping to reveal the book I bought for her a few weeks ago.

"The Adventure of Sherlock Holmes? Oh! I've heard great things about this book."

I waited patiently as she opened the cover. I knew the moment she spotted my note to her, as moisture gathered in the corner of her eyes. She held a hand over her heart as she read the words out loud.

"Dearest Dory, Happy Birthday. I hope you enjoy this book for many years to come. All my... Love. Greyson."

She sniffed as she set the book down. Then she retrieved a handkerchief and dabbed at the corner of her eyes.

"Do you really mean it?"

I reached over and took her hand. Then I lifted it to my lips and kissed it. "Very much."

Her green eyes shimmered. "This is the nicest gift I've ever received."

My mouth quirked in a half-smile as I could hardly wait to hear what she thought of my next gift.

Then she leaned toward me and placed a kiss on my cheek. "Thank you. I love it."

The server arrived with our food, so I took Dory's hand and prayed over the meal, thanking God for her, our shared birthday, and for the food.

"I feel a little bad," she said. "I didn't purchase a gift for you. Just baked a cake."

"You've already given me the only gift I truly desired: this time with you tonight."

Pink dusted her cheeks as she ate a bite of her meal.

"Tell me about your family," she said.

"I have one younger brother, Dawson, and my mother. Both live on the family ranch near Flagstaff. My father passed when I was sixteen."

"Nine years ago?"

I nodded. "I knew how to run the ranch and teach my brother. The things I didn't know, I learned from Mama or our foreman."

"Do you miss them?"

"I do. I thought I would only be gone for a year. Now, I'm not so sure if I'll go back."

"Why not?"

I wasn't ready to delve into that as it depended largely on her.

"The timing isn't right. When I'm ready, I'll make sure your father has time to hire someone else."

She took a sip of water. "You don't want Larson Stables?"

I sighed. "It was gracious of your parents to offer that, given the circumstances. However, I would like to go back to my home. It was always my intention to purchase more horses and start breeding and training. I just lost my dreams somewhere along the way."

"I would miss you if you were to leave."

I wanted to reassure her I would only leave if she came with me. But it was too soon.

Instead, I reached up to brush the back of my fingers across her cheek. "I'm not going anywhere soon."

When she turned her face to press her lips against my hand, my heart rate sped up. Yeah, I wouldn't leave without her.

I withdrew my second gift for her from my jacket pocket. Then I handed it to her.

When she quirked an eyebrow, I winked. "Open it."

As the brown paper slipped off the small box, she carefully lifted the lid to reveal the gold locket. She opened the locket to find no pictures.

"I think you should decide what pictures go in the locket. Your parents or your sisters. Or whomever."

"Will you help me put it on?"

"Gladly."

I stood and took the locket from her slender fingers. Then I unfastened it and rested it against her soft skin. My hand brushed against her neck as I fastened it again. I rested my hand on her silky shoulder as her fingers touched the closed locket. Then she craned her neck to look up at me.

"I love it."

After I paid for the meal, I helped her rise to her feet and placed her shawl over her shoulders. Then I escorted her home, content with everything about her and the night.

"Come in for some cake?" she asked.

"Of course."

When we entered the house, Adam greeted me. His brow wrinkled as Dory dished up the birthday cake.

"While you were gone, this came." He slid a telegram across the table to me.

As I unfolded the paper and read the words, my throat constricted.

Dawson sick. Need help.

I drummed my fingers on the table. This could not be happening. I wasn't ready to leave Dory. But the message was obvious. Mama needed me to go home.

When Dory set a piece of cake in front of me, I clasped her hand. She looked down into my eyes as I cleared my throat.

"I... Have to go home."

CHAPTER 10

DORY

GREYSON'S WORDS LANDED on my heart with a crushing weight. A dozen questions rolled through my mind as I bit my lip and searched his eyes. Was everything alright? How long would he be gone? Would he forget about me?

My gaze slid away from his.

"It's my brother. He's sick and Mama needs my help."

I turned away, but his hold on my hand tightened as he stood. He walked with me to the kitchen. When he faced me, my eyes burned. I didn't want him to go, even though I understood he had to.

"Dory," his whisper wrapped around my heart like a warm blanket. "I don't want to leave. But I must. Mama can't manage the ranch on her own."

The moisture in the corner of my eyes spilled over as fear squeezed my heart. My fingers flew to the locket around my neck. Surely I could trust his feelings for me. The book and necklace proved it.

"I wish I could bring you with me." His voice remained low and soothing. "I love you. I want…"

The words faded, and I sniffed as my eyes found his again. For several seconds, I searched his eyes for the truth. He loved me.

"I love you, too." My voice cracked.

Then he pulled me into his arms as I cried against his chest. He rubbed soothing circles on my back as he rested his chin on the top of my head. I loved him. He loved me. Would he still feel the same when he returned home?

"Hey," he said as he leaned back. "I will write to you as often as I can. I will miss you every day."

With a finger under my chin, he lifted my face to look into my eyes. "I *will* come back for you. That I promise."

Then he brushed a soft kiss across my lips before he stepped back. His hands clasped mine.

"What do you say we enjoy the cake you baked for us? Then we can sit and talk if you'd like."

I nodded as he released my hands. He carried the piece of cake to the table. Then he held out the chair and scooted it in as I sat down.

When Greyson took a bite of the cake, he closed his eyes and hummed.

"This is so good. You've outdone yourself again."

Heat warmed my cheeks. "Thank you."

As I ate my piece, Greyson discussed his plans to pack that night and take the first train north in the morning. Sadness shaded the otherwise perfect evening. I would miss him more than I could say.

———

GREYSON HAD BEEN gone for a week. I wore the locket from him every day. After I placed a loaf of bread in the oven and washed my hands, I touched the locket as I prayed for him. I missed him terribly.

"Dory!" My cousin Sam called my name as he opened the door.

"This came for you."

I frowned at the paper. "A telegram?"

He thrust it toward me and left.

As I read the words on the page, they blurred.

Greyson sick. Asking for Dory.

I wiped my tears on my apron and hurried out to the corral. When Mama saw me, she jogged to meet me.

"What is it?"

I handed her the paper. Within seconds, she pulled me into a hug.

"Can I go?"

"Of course, sweetheart. Of course."

As I pulled away from her embrace, I blotted my face dry.

"You go pack. I'll talk to your father."

The muscles in my neck tightened as I ran back to the house. It must be bad if his family wired me. *Lord, please help.* I couldn't think of anything else to say as I stuffed another dress and nightgown into a valise. My hands grabbed toiletries, a brush, and who knew what else as I worried about him. Then my gaze snagged on the book from Greyson. I stuffed it in the bag.

A few minutes later, Papa entered the house.

"I have a horse saddled for you. We'll ride into town together."

I followed him outside. He gave me a hand up. Then we rode fast to the train station. Thankfully, we arrived with plenty of time to catch the next train to Flagstaff.

"I don't know where his ranch is."

"I'll come with you, and I won't return home until I know you're settled."

"Thanks Papa."

He paid the ticket master for our fares and that of our horses. Then I waited impatiently until the train pulled into the station. The ride to Flagstaff took a few hours. I continued to pray as I watched the landscape fly by. Had I not been so worried about Greyson, it may have registered in my mind that it was my first train ride. Nothing besides Greyson mattered.

By mid-afternoon, Papa and I found the Hastings' ranch, nestled in a grassy valley in the shadow of tall pine trees. Mount Humphreys stood tall in the distance. Had I not been so fretful, I might have enjoyed the beauty of Greyson's home.

Papa tied the horses to a post. Then he knocked on the ranch house's door.

After a minute, a woman slowly opened the door. Streaks of silver lightened her otherwise dark hair. When she sucked in a breath, she coughed. Once the fit subsided, she offered a weak smile.

"Dory?"

"Yes, Mrs. Hastings. This is my father, Adam Larson."

"Please come in. And call me Isabel."

She offered us a seat at the table before she set a kettle on the stove.

"Where is Greyson?" I asked.

Another round of coughs shook her body. She gripped the edge of the counter. I quickly stood and helped her to a chair. Then I waited for the water to boil and made us tea.

"He's very sick. I'm just starting to feel better myself."

I held back a snort. The dark circles under her eyes and the slump of her shoulders rounding forward contradicted her words.

When I set the steaming cup in front of her, she squeezed my hand.

"Thank you for coming. Dawson is barely on the mend. We've all been miserable."

"Well, I'm here now. I will help in whatever way I can."

After we finished the tea, Papa pulled me aside. "Will you be alright if I head home? Or do you want me to stay?"

A young man entered the house. His dark eyes reminded me of Greyson. His medium brown hair looked disheveled. He slunk toward a chair in the living room and collapsed in it.

"You must be Dawson," I said before I introduced myself and my father.

He nodded.

"Do you need help with the stock?" Papa asked.

"No. Between myself and our foreman, we're able to keep up with them."

Papa turned toward me. "I'll stable your horse. Then I'm going to head home."

"Alright. I'll send word as soon as I can."

He kissed my cheek and left.

Then I helped Isabel back to bed before I entered Greyson's room. My breath caught in my throat when I saw his ashen face. Dark circles rested under his eyes. All the vibrancy of the man I loved had disappeared.

A tear slid down my cheek. Then I sat on the edge of his bed and held his hand.

"I'm here, Greyson."

He moaned and his eyes barely opened. "Dory."

My heart broke. He seemed so frail and weak.

"Hush now. I'm here. I'll get you back on your feet soon."

When he fell asleep again, I returned to the kitchen. I sent Dawson to bed. Then I inventoried their supplies and started a pot of chicken stew, reserving some of the rich stock for Greyson.

As the aroma filled the house, both Dawson and Isabel came out to the dining room. I poured the stock into a mug. Then I returned to Greyson's side, figuring they could dish up the stew for themselves.

"Greyson, can you sit up?" I asked as I set the mug on the small table next to his bed.

He moaned. "Dory?"

"I'm here."

Once he leaned forward, I propped another pillow behind him. Then I held the mug to his lips. He sipped the warm liquid.

"You came."

"Of course," I said, as I dampened a cloth and wiped his forehead.

After he finished the mug of broth, his energy faded, and he sank against the pillows again. I pulled the blankets up to his chin. Then I kissed his forehead and returned to the main part of the house.

Over the following days, I spent my time cooking, cleaning, and caring for Greyson. Isabel and Dawson appeared much improved after two days. Greyson's recovery seemed slower. In the afternoons, I sat in a chair in his room and read to him from *The Adventures of Sherlock Holmes*.

One afternoon, I suddenly felt warm and clammy. Waves of exhaustion washed over me. When I stood to start supper, dizziness overtook me, and I dropped to the floor. Sleep beckoned me under.

CHAPTER 11

GREYSON

I WOKE TO the sound of a loud thump. When I glanced around my room, my heart raced at the sight of Dory on the floor, unconscious.

"Mama!" I hollered as I leapt from the bed, barely registering how much energy flowed through me.

She opened the door. "Oh, my! Can you carry her?"

As I crouched down, coughs shook my body. Once the fit ended, I asked if Dawson was around. A few minutes later, with his help, we settled Dory in my bed. Mama said she'd been sleeping on the sofa in the living room.

Mama brought her things into my room. I grabbed a change of clothes, then headed to the washroom for a long overdue bath, leaving the love of my life in my mother's care.

She came. Dory came. I knew she loved me. Probably had for much longer than I loved her.

I thought back to the night I overheard her words on the dock. She prayed for me. The desire of her heart was for me to love her in return.

"Oh, Dory."

Her name left my lips on a breath. I loved her so much more

than I could have imagined. When I first arrived back home, as I took care of the ranch, my brother, and my mother, my thoughts often turned toward Dory. She belonged at my side. As my wife.

As I dressed in clean clothes, I prayed for her. *Lord, please let her heal quickly. I can't lose her. She means everything to me. I want her to be my wife. She is my soulmate. I was foolish not to have seen it sooner.*

I took a deep breath. Then I entered the main part of the house.

"She's resting comfortably," Mama said. "She woke long enough for me to help her into something more comfortable."

I nodded.

"How are you feeling?" she asked.

"Better. A little tired. You?"

"The cough lingers but, I don't feel tired all the time. I'm able to get through most of my regular chores."

"Dawson?"

Mama snorted. "You wouldn't even know he'd been sick."

A half smile broke across my lips.

"You love her, don't you?"

I nodded.

"With all my heart."

"What about Penny?"

As I sipped a tea, I glanced up at Mama. "I think I liked the idea of a wife more than actually loving her. What I feel for Dory is so much deeper. When I picture the future, Dory is always there. She is wonderful, everything I didn't know I wanted in a wife."

Mama smiled. "Well, we'll do our best to get her back on her feet. Pray for her son."

"I am."

———

DAYS TURNED INTO a week. I wired the Larsons to let them know Dory had been sick but improved. In the afternoon, I sat with her, reading the Sherlock Holmes book. She felt a little better each day. In a few more days, she'd be well enough to return home.

When I worked with the cattle or horses, I thought about her. Though it was time to remain at my family's ranch and start building my horse business, I wanted Dory to stay with me forever.

One afternoon, she joined me in the barn. While her cough still sounded bad, mine disappeared at last.

"Afternoon," I greeted her with a smile. "Are you up for a ride?"

"I think so. A short one."

She watched as I saddled Shadow and Cookie. Then I helped her up before I climbed onto Shadow. A few minutes later, we rode a trail on my property that wove through tall pine trees.

"It's so beautiful here," she said. "While you were sick, I often sat on the porch just taking in the sight."

"I'm glad you like it. I forgot how much I missed being here."

Dory rode next to me. When her smile faded, my heart squeezed tight.

"You aren't coming back with me, are you?" she asked.

Long enough to marry, I hoped. Not the time for that revelation yet. I sighed as I turned in my saddle to watch her. "I'll see you safely home. But I will need to return here."

A tear slipped from the corner of her eye. "I don't want to go."

Love rushed over me. I pulled my horse to a stop. Then I helped her down before I pulled her against me, reins in one hand. I searched her eyes before I lowered my lips to hers, expressing how much I longed to keep her there.

At length, I slowed the kiss. Then I rested my forehead against hers.

"I love you, Dory."

"Oh, Greyson, please don't send me home."

Perhaps it was time to ask.

CHAPTER 12

DORY

WHEN GREYSON TOLD me he loved me, my heart broke in two. I didn't want to leave his side. He wanted to stay in Flagstaff. My home was near Prescott. Only one thing would allow me to stay with him forever.

He tied the horses to a tree. Then he led me to a downed tree to use as a bench. Before I knew it, he dropped to one knee.

"Dory, I love you with all my heart and soul. You are beautiful, the only love of my life, and the only one for me. Will you marry me? I don't have a ring for you yet, but I will soon."

His handsome face blurred in my vision as I placed my hands on each side of his face. Then I leaned close.

"Yes! A thousand times, yes!"

The words barely left my lips before he crushed me against him, his lips capturing mine with the most delicious kiss. My heart swelled with love for him, the only man for me, the desire of my heart.

As the kiss ended, I rested my head against his chest and wrapped my arms around his middle. He stroked my hair with one hand as the other rested at my waist.

"I'll ask your father for his permission when we arrive."

"Will you come back here? When will we marry?" I asked, desperate to become his wife.

"If you think your family might agree, perhaps we could marry in a week or two. So when I come back here, you'll join me."

I leaned away from him. "I'd love nothing more."

———

ON JUNE THIRTIETH, Greyson and I stood on the dock before my large extended family. It was a beautiful, sunny afternoon. Caty and Penny stood with me as I faced Greyson and promised to love and obey him until death parted us. His brother Dawson and my cousin Sam stood next to him as he promised to cherish and love me forever.

When the pastor introduced us as Mr. and Mrs. Greyson Hastings, he kissed me until I grew lightheaded. As we started walking back down the pier, my balance felt off.

"Careful, Mrs. Hastings. I wouldn't want you to fall into the lake on your wedding day," Greyson teased me.

"Kiss me like that again, and I might."

His hearty laughter echoed across the lake. My husband and love.

As we made our way to the large makeshift picnic table in the shade of a cottonwood tree, I thought back to my starry night prayers. God granted me many of the desires of my heart. He gave me Greyson as a husband. A godly man like my father, who loved me as much as my father loved my mother. How unlikely it would have been to stand there as Greyson's wife had he not overheard my prayers that night.

"God works in mysterious ways," I said as Greyson held a

chair out for me.

"Indeed, He does," he whispered as he placed a kiss on my cheek.

Once Papa said a beautiful blessing over us and the meal, we started eating.

"Greyson, I think I've decided I want a picture of my sisters for the locket."

"I'll see to it," he said. "Looks like each Larson daughter ended up with the man of her dreams."

I glanced over at Penny, four months pregnant. Both Caty and I squealed with delight when she shared the good news. I would be an aunt again. I wondered how long before Greyson and I might have similar news.

"She looks so happy with him," Greyson said as he nodded toward Penny and Nathan. "And I'm so happy with you, Dory. You are truly my soulmate. If Nathan hadn't shown up last year, what would have happened?"

"Best not to dwell on the past, my love. Things worked out as they should have."

Greyson clasped my hand for a second. "So wise."

After a few bites of food, my new husband turned to me. "You know, I'm kind of glad I found you out on the pier on Valentine's Day."

I laughed. "You are?"

"Of course. I'm sorry you fell in, but I'm not sorry I overheard you. It's the moment that woke me up to you. You are perfect for me."

"Well, I suppose if that's what it took..." I winked at him.

He beamed and waggled his eyebrows before he stole another kiss from me.

"Yeah, I don't regret that night one minute."

EPILOGUE

July 3, 1899

GREYSON

"Dory!" I shook my wife awake just after midnight. She groaned.

"Come on, sweet wife. Wake up."

"I'm tired."

"I know you are. But I have a surprise for you."

As she slung her feet over the side of the guest bed in her parents' house, I held up a robe for her. She stood, and I slid it over her arms before I wrapped it around her extended belly. Like I so often did, I paused a moment to rest my hands over where our second child grew.

"Do you believe this will be a boy or girl?" I asked.

"Will you be disappointed if she's another girl?"

"Not even a little."

"Good."

When I released Dory, I offered my arm and led her outside into the dark night. Not even the moon lit our path. Good thing I grabbed a lantern.

"Careful," I warned her as we stepped over the threshold of the dock.

"Greyson, I don't think I could stand up if you have me sit on the dock."

"Not to worry. I figured as much."

I led her to the rocking chairs I set near the end of the pier. Once she sat, I put the lantern down before I sat in the other rocker. Then I clasped her hand and looked up at the beautiful starry night sky.

"What do we do next?" I whispered.

Dory giggled. "I'm not sure. I've only told my deepest secrets to my sisters and God. A man has never been part of the conversation."

I laughed. "At least not intentionally."

"True."

She dropped her head back to gaze at the stars. I did the same. For many minutes, we sat there quietly, looking up.

Soft snores came from the chair next to me. My dear wife fell asleep. I wouldn't hold it against her. Her time to deliver our second child was only a month away. I was glad we could make the trip down to her parents' place. It was only a few days after our fifth anniversary. Even though we spent some holidays with her family, this was the first time I brought her out to the dock.

"Oh! I'm sorry," she whispered. "I didn't mean to dose off."

I rubbed my thumb over the back of her hand. "Let me pray, then I'll take you back to bed."

"Lord, thank you for your magnificent starry night sky and the way You used it to bring us together. May you bless the Hastings and Larson families for generations to come. Thank you for my beautiful wife and our daughter. Keep this coming baby safe. Help him know he's loved by You and by his parents."

"Her."

"Or her. Amen."

After a few more minutes, I stood. As we walked back to the house, I was full of more love for her than the day we married. And forever grateful for her tradition of stargazing with her sisters, even after they all left home. It was my favorite part of our story.

AUTHOR'S NOTE

After spending the fall reading several Christmas novels and novellas, I was inspired to write one of my own. When I looked through my sheet of potential matches for minor characters from other books, I thought it might be nice to tell the Larson sisters' stories as a set of novellas.

Like all my series, I wanted something unique to these women, besides sisterhood, to connect the series together. I began thinking about how three very close sisters might share their secrets.

After taking a trip up to Prescott in the fall, I remembered how the stars are clearly visible at night, which is so different from the big city I live in. My mind began to fit the pieces together. What if the Larson sisters liked to stargaze and share their secrets? Viola! The Larson Sisters Novellas began to take shape.

I chose the shorter novella format for a few reasons, the primary one being that I had several other full-length novels in process, some with hard deadlines. My intention with the Larson sisters was to focus solely on romance. No action. No adventure. Something different from the Colter Sons series. So, I needed to keep it concise. I also thought readers might enjoy an easy way to try out books as a new-to-them author.

When I first introduced Caty (Catherine) Larson in the Prescott Pioneers Series, I never intended to shorten her name. Yet, I shortened Penelope to Penny and Dolores to Dory in the Colter Sons Series. So, I needed a shortened version of Catherine that would look nice in the title. I know. It's a silly reason. Caty fit, so I went with it.

Anyway, I hope you enjoyed reading the three sisters' love stories in this format.

Thanks for your continued support!

Karen Baney

About the Author

Karen Baney is passionate about writing stories full of flawed characters. She enjoys weaving together stories of second chances, redemption, and overcoming personal trials. As a transplant to Arizona, she loves researching the state's history and finding ways to seamlessly incorporate real history and real settings into her novels. In addition to writing and speaking, Karen works as a Software Development Manager for a Christian ministry.

Her faith plays an important role both in her life and in her writing. Karen and her husband, Jim, make their home in Gilbert, Arizona, with their two dogs, Bella and Daisy. Both Jim and Karen are active at Rock Point Church in Queen Creek, Arizona.

Discover faith-laced stories with characters who feel like lifelong friends.

Visit www.karenbaney.com to discover more historical romance series set in the American West. Follow Karen's writing journey and get behind-the-scenes glimpses of her research adventures on social media.

Facebook: @AuthorKarenBaney
X: @karen_baney
Instagram: @AuthorKarenBaney
BookBub: Follow Karen Baney for new release alerts

BOOKS BY KAREN BANEY

Historical Western Romance

Step back in time to the wild, untamed Arizona Territory where survival depends on grit, faith, and the courage to start over. Follow three pioneer families—the Andersons, Colters, and Larsons—as they risk everything for the promise of a new life in a land that demands both strength and hope.

A Dream Unfolding
A Heart Renewed
A Life Restored
A Hope Revealed
Hidden Prospects

Sometimes the most beautiful love stories bloom in the desert. Set in the growing frontier town of Prescott during the early

1870s, these tender romances follow women rebuilding their lives after heartbreak and the unexpected men who help them discover that second chances at love are worth the risk. Set in Prescott, Arizona between 1871 - 1873.

Beauty for Ashes
Joy for Mourning
Oaks of Justice

Power, legacy, and forbidden love collide in this sweeping family saga set in the Arizona Territory. The Colter ranch empire has weathered decades of frontier life, but now family secrets and buried betrayals threaten to destroy everything. As five brothers—and one resilient sister—navigate the treacherous waters of love, loss, and redemption, they must decide what's worth fighting for. Set in Prescott and other locations within the Arizona Territory in 1887 - 1906.

The Reluctant Cattleman
The Roaming Adventurer
The Railroad Magnate
The Resourceful Stockman
The Restless Wrangler
The Resilient Bride

Meet the next generation! These delightful novellas follow the three daughters of Adam and Julia Larson from the *Prescott Pioneers Series* as they navigate love, courtship, and finding their own happily ever-afters in territorial Arizona in 1886 – 1894.

In Love at Christmas
In Love with the Rancher
In Love with the Horse Trainer

Contemporary Romance

Love is in the air at the Vargas Guest Ranch & Resort near Wickenburg, Arizona. Meet the Vargas family—five swoon-worthy brothers and their cousins who live by their family motto: "We do not deviate from the Lord's plan." These rugged cowboys run a successful working ranch and luxury resort while navigating the rollercoaster of finding true love.

Falling for a Fake Cowboy
Falling for a Real Cowboy
Honeymoon with a Real Cowboy
Falling for a Shy Cowboy
Falling for a Bossy Cowboy
Falling for a Smart Cowboy
Falling for a Humbug Cowboy
Falling for a Devoted Cowgirl
Falling for a Pregnant Cowgirl
Falling for a Cowboy's Legacy

Steadfast Love Series

The *Steadfast Love* series follows a close-knit group of friends as they navigate the beautiful mess of modern life in the Phoenix area—workplace drama, complicated families, and love that shows up when they least expect it. These contemporary romances blend emotional depth with authentic faith, reminding us that even when life unravels, God's love never does.

The Heart I Rescue (prequel)
The Air I Breathe

DESERT LIFE MEDIA

———

Desert Life Media: *There Is Life in The Desert*

Entertainment-first Christian fiction set in the Southwest, featuring redemption, family, and faith

Publishing clean, wholesome, and uplifting fiction since 2010

———

desertlifemedia.com

www.ingramcontent.com/pod-product-compliance
Lightning Source LLC
Chambersburg PA
CBHW051953220626
47052CB00004B/931